Burials and other stories

Rob McInroy

Ringwood Publishing

Glasgow

Copyright Rob McInroy© 2024
All rights reserved

The moral right of the author has been asserted

Ringwood Publishing
0/1 314 Meadowside Quay Walk, Glasgow G11 6AY

www.ringwoodpublishing.com
mail@ringwoodpublishing.com

ISBN 978-1-917011-06-8

British Library Cataloguing-in-Publication Data
A catalogue record for this book is available from the
British Library

Printed and bound in the UK
by Lonsdale Direct Solutions

Contents

Fair Near a Riverside Town (after Jan Steen) 1
(In My Way) 7
Burials 9
Fresh Watter 25
The Entertainer 37
A Curious Judgement 51
Brainspotting 59
Joss'n'Jules Forever 67
Peewit 73
Sequela 75
The Rational Matters of Rational Men 81
Man Walks Into A Bar 95
The White Deer 97
The Woman Who Called Herself Karen 103
Taking Tea With The Other Woman 111
Not Drowning Yet 115
The Weight of Snow 125
Oysters and Ink 133
Evanescence 141
Whisky Night 153
About the Stories 159
Acknowledgements 161
About the Author 163

For my sister, Lynne D'Agostino
The best big sister I could have.

Fair Near a Riverside Town (after Jan Steen)

Crieff at play, bifurcated. *I'm a rover, seldom sober. Amazing grace, how sweet the sound.* Drink to the glory, drunkards of past and present times. Families gather, peace and harmony. Soft wind and no rain, and in it the tribes of Crieff congregate. Have some fun. Have a care.

Ash and old man Disdain and Emily and Jack walked through the shows. Mid-afternoon, the throng would grow worse later but it was busy enough now. Jack bristled as people walked behind him. *Leave me space. Don't crowd me.* Ash, the American, was presented with a toffee apple and bit it triumphantly, disguising the fact it tasted horrible. Emily, too, was given one. Born to such confections, she appreciated it more. At the shooting stall, Jack tried his luck and won a yellow gonk and presented it to Emily. Ash challenged him to aim for a bigger prize. A giant teddy bear was identified and the transaction explained – five perfect rounds of three shots on target. Jack negotiated the first three rounds with ease, then the fourth more slowly. Tension, pressure, and Jack unused to such affairs.

Ash paid the stallholder and took up a rifle of her own and held out her hand for the three feathered pellets. Jack hit bullseye once more. Two more for the teddy. He flexed his fingers, aimed and squeezed the trigger. Missed.

'No,' he said, crestfallen.

'No,' said Ash. She took aim across the stall and fired and holed the centre of Jack's target. 'No,' she repeated. 'Jes one more.'

And Jack aimed and fired and holed the centre.

'Hurrah,' shouted Ash. 'Hey,' she called to the stallholder, pointing at Jack's target. 'We won.' Unclear how he had been duped but certain he had, the stallholder handed over the teddy with ill grace. Jack gave it to Ash and smiled. Achievement. File it in the memory for days less happy than this, Jack.

A small child, little more than an urchin, dressed in dungarees and yellow tee-shirt, fell into a puddle on the rugby pitch and began to cry. Emily picked it up – girl, mop-headed, dirty and cute at the same time. She smiled at Emily's ministrations, curious, unused to attention. A parent emerged, full of alcohol and seething repression, and claimed the child and Emily made her farewells and handed her back to authority. 'Here,' she said, and gave her the gonk. The afternoon progressed.

Ash stood before the waltzers. They rocked round and round in a clockwise circle while the stall hands grabbed each carriage and wheeled it in the opposite direction. Girls screamed. Boys screamed.

'Who's comin on with me?' she said. No volunteer spoke up. She grabbed Emily's hand and dragged her to the entrance and paid the fee to a man in dirty overalls and they were strapped into a chair by a younger man. Handsome. Pretty smile, full of teeth.

And the ride turned and the afternoon turned with it. Heat threatened, briefly, sunshine and little wind. On the rugby pitch the Kinross Majorettes gave a spangly performance. Kester Dunning appreciated lasciviously, unafraid to let others, distaff others, discern the shape of that appreciation beneath his trousers. Faces confronted, searching kindredness. No takers, not yet. The others found a spot on the rugby pitch and laid out Emily's blanket. Chips and beans from the stalls. Bob Kelty sidled by with his bagpipes, promising music later. Picnic neighbours, families and the elderly, unwrapped tin foil or cling film to reveal sandwiches, boiled eggs, sausage rolls, *al fresco* assortments hallowed through the ages. Experienced in managing wind and rain and midge and earwig, balancing cups, protecting plates, they settled into an afternoon's recreation.

'Sorry I'm late.' They squinted up to see Mally Vogel standing in front of them. He was not sober. 'I got waylaid by a couple of Mormons.'

'In the Drummond Arms?' said the old man.

'Commissioner Street.'

'You shouldn't be here,' said Jack. 'Restraining order.'

'Fuck that,' said Mally. 'There's hundreds here. Who's going to spot me in this crowd?'

'As long as you don't make a spectacle of yourself.'

Walking on Sunshine began to play over the tannoy, tinny and hissing and uninviting. 'I fucking hate this song,' said Mally. 'How are you supposed to dance to that?'

'You can dance to that,' said Ash.

'Not without making an arse of yourself.'

Ash stood and wiped sugary hands on her knees and started to dance, arms stretching out and fingers flexing. Her hips swung and swayed and she pirouetted in a sinuous dance, loose-limbed, elegant. Emily watched, smiling. The old man smoked a Marlboro. Ash bent low and raised herself high, rocking on her heels, gesturing to the group, twisting and turning, walking on sunshine.

'Okay,' said Mally. He leapt to his feet and began to mimic her actions. It was horrible. Where there was grace now was coarseness, a simian galumph, inelegant, awkward, inept. He fell twice. A crowd gathered, laughed.

'As long as he don't make a spectacle of himself,' said Ash.

Afternoon into evening. Imperceptibly, the mood changed. Families departed in tempers and tears. The average age decreased. Noise increased. Mally drank whisky from a hip flask. The old man smoked Marlboro in relays. It was only seven o'clock but already lights were beginning to glow, reds and greens and blues and yellows around the show rides and stalls, orange from the streetlights, sterile white from temporary floodlights at the car park and walkways. Roar of generator, diesel smell. The river Earn ran in colours of the rainbow, quiet and slow, sedate out of the wind. Occasional flashes of yellow revealed recalcitrant plastic shapes still negotiating that afternoon's duck race from Comrie.

And so the evening rolled on. Darkness fell on Braidhaugh. Bob Kelty stood in the centre of the rugby pitch and looked over into the blanket of evening and started to play his pipes and he played a lament and he thought of Pipey Oldham and he thought of his late wife Annie and he thought of love and he thought of loneliness and he thought of the new generation, new hope, his beautiful granddaughter Emily for whom everything existed, waiting to be revealed, for whom the past is only a story told by her grandpa or her mother or her father and the future is a place as tangible as this and none of the hurt she will experience can yet be known. He played. The world was silent to him, disconnected through choice. He began to pace up and down the centre line, pibroch resolving into the night.

Behind him, under the glare of a giant spotlight, Kester Dunning punched Willie Nicholl and Willie Nicholl punched Kester Dunning. They wrestled, trading blows with more enthusiasm than skill. Mally Vogel pulled a long piece of tubing from his bag and put it to his mouth and fed something into it. He blew. A ragged stranger clapped his hand to his neck and rubbed it. Mally replenished his implement, improvised blowpipe of his own devising. The noise of night reverberated. A chill blew down. Scuffles and skirmishes broke out in patches, rolling around the site and feeding off one another. Individual scraps gradually merged into larger mêlées. Screams and yells filled the night, drowned out the solitary piper in his reverie. A blowpipe dart stuck in the cheek of Kenny McAskill. He howled. Boys from the shows, handy lads, fit, strong, joined the fray. The fray grew. Ash and Emily and Jack and the old man watched. The sound of sirens filtered through the tumult, blue lights flashing, order approaching, reckoning.

'Fascist pigs,' yelled Mally. He fired his final dart at PC Braggan. PC Mitchell forced him into a headlock and marched him to the Panda car. He was handcuffed and bundled into the back and the policemen returned with relish to the scene of engagement. A Black Maria arrived and the crowd began to dissipate, irreproachable fun over, discretion dictating an end to current rivalries. People with weeping eyes and cuts and gouges and grazes sauntered past the assembled officers of the law as though promenading on a Sunday afternoon. The fuss subsided.

'In foolishness,' said Ash, 'time is forgotten.'

On the rugby pitch, Bob Kelty played *Banish Misfortune*. He turned and looked at the shows behind him, quiet in the summer dark, readying for night.

(In My Way)

When I was at school I was the revered (in my head) writer of stories about the bold (in his head) Dobbin F. Lugosi, trainee vampire and admirer of beautiful (in our heads) Dyl Hambone, minx, vixen, vegetarian werewolf. Since Dobbin loved Dyl and he was me and she was Laura the subtext was obvious, at least to me, but neither I nor Dobbin ever managed to get beyond the written word.

Perhaps it was because (in our hearts) we knew that the promise was better than the kiss.

Three years later (all alone) I met Laura in London (with a man). She smiled, I smiled, the dormant Dobbin F. Lugosi awoke. He remembered his beloved Dyl, remembered his broken heart. He threw back his head, cast a baleful gaze at the moon and howled (I love you).

'You still writing?' said Laura. (Dyl didn't deign to appear.) Dobbin and I shook our head(s) in dismay.

Two years later Laura came back from London and we shared air kisses (as adults do). How are you, I said, and she said fine but her eyes said the man was gone.

'I liked those stories,' she said.

'Dobbin and Dyl?'

She nodded. 'They were cool.'

She hadn't aged. Her skin was impossibly smooth, eyes primed for mischief. It was like talking to Dyl Hambone all over again (in my dreams).

'I've still got them,' she said. 'Read them sometimes. They make me laugh.'

(They make me cry.)

'You were good. Don't you still write?'

(I lost my muse.) 'Occasionally, but it's not the same.' (Not the same.)

'I always wanted them to get together at the end.'

(So did I.)

'I always thought they were us.'

(They were.)

(And her hand is in mine as we sit on the beach. She's talking of the past but living in the present. Things merge, it's an alchemical moment. I wish I knew what to do.)

'Didn't you think they should fall in love?' she said. And Dyl caressed Dobbin's arm.

'Of course,' said Dobbin F. Lugosi.

'So why didn't they?'

(Perfection's so much easier on the page: no worries, no failure. If the words don't work, tear them up, start all over again.)

(If love's too raw best keep it in the shade, in the mind, out of the way. It's an aspiration, and Dobbin says it's better to aspire than expire.)

I think Dobbin's full of shit.

'Did you love me, once?' said Dyl, said Laura, said the present to the past. 'I always suspected, but you never said.' She held my hand and we were fused together. Dyl reached out to Dobbin, as she never had before.

'Do you love me still?' And Laura reached out to Jack, as she never had before.

Dyl and Laura, they showed Dobbin and Jack that the promise, however sweet, is only a whisper of the kiss, and what a kiss (they kissed).

'Do you love me?' they said.

In my way.

(In my head.)

Burials

The only thing that was clear was that John O'Brien did not kill Samantha Hedges. On Saturday afternoon he walked unaccompanied into Crieff Police Station and confessed to the murder of the twelve-year-old missing girl whose body had been found the previous afternoon following a six-day search. He stood at the counter and quietly explained to Sergeant Kellaway how he had abducted the girl as she walked home from school, taken her to a remote area of the Knock hill and murdered her, then buried her in a grave covered by several inches of soil and topped with rotting beech leaves.

'I buried her,' he said. 'That's how it should be done.'

Roger Neet and Louise Russell knew something was wrong. Hoax confessions were easy to detect. Because cranks didn't know how the crime was committed they would invent. Get facts wrong. They would repeat false details planted in news reports. They would miss essentials. Eventually, they would descend into fantasy. Their confessions would be logged and they'd be charged with wasting police time. It was an irritant.

But John was different.

His voice was soft, barely modulated. It was difficult to catch his words and the detectives had to ask him several times to speak up for the recording. He continued as though he hadn't heard them. He related again and again how he took the child, how he led her to a patch of woodland near the Witch's Crag, how he killed her and buried her. He retained eye contact with the officers at all times, which was unusual. He appeared unflustered, which was common, but to a degree that unnerved them. During the entire interview he rested his hands, palms upward, on the table. He asked for nothing, never spoke to his appointed brief, barely moved.

'The way the blood pulsed out of her back, it was like a hose spurting water.'

'Tell us more about that,' said Neet.

'It was red and black and purple. It bubbled. It smelled. I didn't expect it to smell. It didn't run away into the ground. You couldn't stop it. It wasn't until I buried her that it went away.'

'You buried her?' said Louise.

'Yes.'

The detectives were left with a dilemma. Their press statement had revealed that the cause of death was a knife wound to the left kidney, so it was unsurprising that John described spurting blood. But the statement also suggested, as a trap for hoaxers, that the body had been left beneath a light covering of leaves when it had, in fact, been buried. Nobody knew that.

Except, it seemed, John.

There was no DNA match. In any case, experience told them it wasn't him. But he had confessed, and he appeared to know unknowable detail. They were frustrated by the impasse. Both had family the victim's age. Each had unsolved cases in their pasts that still haunted them. Shane Groves. Mary Gill. Their names were like a litany of shame and they were damned if they were going to add Samantha Hedges to it.

Louise Russell tried to break the permafrost around John. 'You feel badly about this murder, don't you, John?' she said. 'All of us do. It's a terrible thing. Abusing children. They're supposed to be able to trust us, aren't they? Childhood is that glorious time. Should be. Happiest days. Do you want to talk about that? Tell me about your childhood?'

'I did it,' said John.

'Did you?'

'I've explained it to you.'

'No you haven't. You've *told* us many, many times. But the one thing you specifically haven't done is *explain*. How, John? And why? It seems out of character. You're a young man. Intelligent. Quiet. Good job. Do you see the trouble I have? I look at you and don't see a cold-hearted killer.'

'It wasn't a cold-hearted killing.'

'Is there another sort? Can you get warm-hearted killers?'

'But that's it exactly.'

'You're a warm-hearted killer?'

'Yes.'

Neet swore. 'I'll be sure to tell Mr and Mrs Hedges that,' he said. 'It'll make it much better for them.'

'That's what I want you to tell them,' John said, his voice softer than ever.

'What is?' said Russell.

'She didn't die badly.'

'What do you mean, not badly?' There was silence as John looked from Russell to Neet and back again. He seemed to be searching for the words. 'John?'

'I want them to know that I was there and that she wasn't in pain and she wasn't frightened and it didn't hurt.'

'She just died peacefully?'

'Yes.'

Russell shook her head. 'She was murdered, John,' she said. 'It wasn't peaceful.'

'Yes.'

'No.'

John nodded his head vigorously, as though seeking to convince them with his certainty. This was the first time he had displayed any agitation in three hours of interrogation. That was good, thought Russell. Time for some pressure.

'Samantha was a twelve-year-old child who was abducted on the way home from school,' she said. 'She was going back to her family. Mum, dad, sister, dog, two cats. Sister's called Harriet. Aged eight. Grandparents, too. Friends. Loads of them. She was a popular girl. First year of high school. She was taken from outside the school by an assailant unknown and for the next six to ten hours we do not know exactly the course of events. She would have been alone. With a psychotic killer. She would have been very, very afraid. Some terrible things happened to her, John. We know that. Terrible things. Would you like me to explain what they were?'

'She died peacefully.'

'She was taken to a dark wood and repeatedly abused. She suffered a serious and sustained sexual assault. Vaginal and anal. She would have been screaming for her family. Crying for her mummy. Wanting to live. Not wanting to die. And then she was brutally murdered.' Russell could see, finally, flickers of emotion on John's face. 'Then left to rot.'

'It wasn't like that.'

'You weren't there, John. You don't know.'

'It's how I explained it. I was there and she didn't suffer. Tell them.'

'Tell who?'

'The family.'

'The family already know,' said Neet. 'They have to know the details. Unlike perverts like you who just get a kick from it.'

'Have you got some kind of Jesus Christ complex?' said Russell. 'Trying to take the pain of the world on your shoulders? Is that what this is? Are you just trying to protect that family from pain?'

'No.'

'Because if you are, however well intentioned it might be, you're actually increasing their suffering. Don't you see that?'

John lowered his head. 'You can't increase their suffering,' he said. 'It goes on forever. And then it starts again. And then it starts again. You can't change that.'

'So what can you change?'

'She didn't suffer.'

'Is that what you're trying to change?'

'No. She didn't suffer. I did it.'

'I know you didn't do it, John. It's what you did do that worries me.'

John looked up and smiled. Russell watched in amazement as his face transformed itself, as though a mask had been peeled from it. 'John?' she said.

'I killed my brother.'

*

'Tell me about how your brother died.'

Neet and Russell sat forward, straining to hear John's voice. After a ten-minute break during which they detailed Logan and Murray to check John's story, they had recommenced the interview. Russell held a vague hope this might be the breakthrough they needed, but when Neet looked at John's emotionless face he still couldn't detect a murderer within.

'We were just playing.'

'When was this, John?'

'Ten years ago. Eleven. It was the SAI mill they were pulling down at MacRosty Park. It was secured at night by a chain fence but we could get in easily. There was this old laundry room. It had a chute that zigzagged over our heads into the floors above. We would climb into the chute and jam ourselves against the sides. They were metal-lined. We'd twist and pull ourselves up and over the ninety degree turns each floor until we reached the top. We'd hold ourselves steady for as long as we could, until we couldn't hold on any longer and then we'd let go. We'd fly down the chute, battering against the walls and tumbling over the bends until we landed on the laundry room floor...'

'Sounds dangerous.'

'Not really. Not usually.'

'Carry on.'

'I don't know how it happened. Probably through the demolition works. A large slab of metal lining came loose near the bottom of the chute. We never noticed. Simon went up first and I waited at the bottom. I could hear him yelling as he bumped all the way down and finally he rocketed down the chute into the room, and his body sliced through the metal. It tore a massive hole in his side, right up to his intestines. Straight away there was blood all around him. He didn't even know it had happened.

'He said, "I feel a bit funny, I think you better get some help." And...' John stopped.

'And?'

'He died.'

He sat for some moments with his head bowed. They waited. Finally, Russell spoke.

'Why did you tell us about this, John? Is it connected to Samantha?'

'Everything's connected.'

'Maybe so. But how? Do you feel responsible for your brother's death? You said you killed him. But you didn't, did you? It was an accident.'

'Not really.'

'Do you blame yourself?'

'No.'

'I think you do. Why do you blame yourself, John?'

'Because I didn't go for help.'

'What did you do?'

'I ran away.'

'Why did you run away?'

'Because I was scared. All that blood. He was crying. He was dying.'

'And... What happened?'

John's voice was almost inaudible. He had shrunk into himself, staring at the table in front of him, hunched, almost as though he wasn't occupying the same physical space as before. 'It was a week before they found his body. There was a big search, appeals on TV, everything. I said nothing. I couldn't.'

Russell pressed forward in her seat. 'That must have been agonising, knowing all that time where he was and not being able to tell anyone.'

'Yes.'

'You probably had nightmares?'

'All the time. He kept coming to me in dreams. Standing over me. Staring.'

'And this child, Samantha Hedges, she was missing for a long time, too, wasn't she? Six days. Did that make you think about Simon?'

'Not really.'

'Not really?' This man was hermetically sealed, she thought. He was suffering some huge mental trauma and he had no way of explaining it. She doubted even he knew what it was, not fully, so deep had he buried it in his psyche. She studied his face, his soft, full mouth and aquiline nose, fine eyelashes, beautiful, longer than hers, and those curious, mismatched eyes, one blue, the other a multi-coloured blue-grey. He was enigmatic. He seemed small, somehow. All of him seemed small. He was a tall man, over six feet, and yet he seemed... diminished. *Compressed.*

'You were only a child,' she said. 'Frightened. I can understand how you must have felt. And I can understand how you must feel now. Are you very lonely, John?'

He nodded.

'Are you angry? With yourself?'

He nodded.

'When you read about the murder of Samantha Hedges, how did that make you feel?'

'I don't remember.'

'Did it make you feel more angry? More lonely? Did it remind you of Simon? How old was Simon when he died?'

'Thirteen.'

'About the same age as Samantha.'

'Yes.'

'Is this confession about guilt transference, John? Because you feel guilty about Simon? If it is, we could all understand that, couldn't we?' Russell gave him an encouraging smile. Neet remained motionless, watching.

John looked at her. 'There's no smoke without fire,' he said.

'What do you mean?'

He closed his eyes. He opened them again and looked around him as though uncertain where he was.

'What do you mean by that?' she repeated. But the connection was gone. John had withdrawn.

There was a knock on the interview room door and Logan entered and whispered into Neet's ear. Neet shook his head.

'Well,' he said. 'Guilt transference? Confessing to a murder because you feel guilt about the death of your brother all those years ago? That's what you're suggesting, is it?' He scraped his chair across the floor and rose stiffly. Russell followed suit. 'Enough of this crap.' He reached towards the tape recorder. 'Interview ends, three thirty-eight. You see, John, the trouble is you never had a brother. You're an only child.'

*

They watched John on the CCTV. He sat on the cot in his cell, knees up, hands clasped, and stared straight ahead.

'He's a fantasist,' said Neet. 'Pure and simple. He didn't

kill the girl. Get rid of him.'

'How did he know she was buried, then?'

'Lucky guess.'

'I agree he didn't kill the girl. But there's something there. He's hiding something.' Eliminate the impossibles, she thought, isolate the improbables, eventually you emerge at the truth. The trouble was everything with John was either impossible or improbable. He didn't stack up. There was a piece of him missing.

'He's just a nutcase,' said Neet. 'I mean, why would he lie about his brother? A brother he hasn't got. He knew he couldn't get away with it. Only a nutter would say that.'

'But that story, it's so detailed. Precise. Convoluted, even. Who would invent that?'

'Well, he obviously did, since it didn't happen.'

'So why?'

There was a knock on the office door and PC Logan entered with an email print-out. She handed it to Neet. He read it and threw it on the table in front of him.

'New analysis from the lab,' he said. 'We appear to have a DNA match after all.'

Russell studied the email. 'That doesn't make sense,' she said. 'That's trivial.'

'It means he was there.'

'But not that he killed her. There's a trace of his DNA on her blouse and her shoes. That's all.'

'So there's somebody else.'

'They don't usually work in pairs.'

'Unusual. But not unknown.'

Russell frowned. The DNA match created more problems than it provided answers. John was definitely there. But he didn't rape Samantha Hedges. Which made it unlikely he killed her, either. So who did? And what was John's involvement? She stared at him in the CCTV camera again. 'Who are you, John O'Brien? What are you running from?'

*

'Interview commencing seven forty-five. Detectives Neet and Russell in attendance. Ms Carrington acting for Mr O'Brien. John O'Brien, your DNA has been identified on the clothing of Samantha Hedges. When I advised you of this development I strongly recommended that you speak with your solicitor. Have you in fact done that?'

Lianne Carrington shook her head.

'For the tape, Ms Carrington indicates that her client has declined to discuss anything relating to this investigation with her. That isn't smart, John. You could get life for this.'

'Good.'

'Who did you do it with?' John looked confused. 'Your accomplice, John.'

'No-one. I did it myself.'

'John, there's a barrel-load of spunk inside that body and none of it is yours. So unless you killed her and buried her, and some nasty man came along afterwards and dug her up again and then had his way with her, which you must accept is highly unlikely, that tends to suggest you had an accomplice.' John remained silent. 'Your accomplice, John. Name?'

'Me.'

'Your DNA has been discovered on the school uniform worn by Samantha Hedges. Specifically her blouse and her shoes. Can you explain how it got there?'

'When I killed her.'

'Why would there only be DNA on her blouse and shoes? The person who killed her also sexually assaulted her. Why is there none of your DNA on the rest of her clothing or her body?'

'No bodily fluids were exchanged.'

'Exactly. It's one of the prerequisites of sexual intercourse, the exchange of bodily fluids. Where are yours?'

'On the blouse and shoes.'

'You didn't fuck her shoes.'

Russell shook her head. 'The thing is, John, the amount of DNA we've found, it isn't enough. It puts you in contact with the body but it doesn't necessarily link you to the murder.' She paused and stared at him. 'Were you just the sidekick?' she said. 'Were you along for the ride?'

John slumped back in his chair. For the first time he lifted his hands from the table. He rested them on his thighs and stared at the opposite wall and told them he had taken Samantha into the woods and killed her.

'She was raped,' said Neet.

John shook his head.

'Anally.'

'I killed her.'

Neet threw down his pen. 'This is pointless,' he said. 'Interview adjourned. Eight twenty-seven.'

The detectives sat in their office and stared at the evidence wall. Frustration spilled over into anger and they argued bitterly about the DNA match and what it meant.

Neet smoked his pen like a cigarette. 'The more I see him, the more I think he's done something bad. Really bad.'

Russell remained silent. She was rapidly coming to the opposite conclusion. This man was massively damaged but, increasingly, she saw fragility rather than violence beneath the blankness of his demeanour. He was concocting an elaborate story around the crime scene, making it safe, vanilla, unthreatening. In his version there was no rape, not even any murder, just a painless, peaceful death. She found it difficult to believe John knew anything of the brutal reality of Samantha's murder.

'Sir?' PC Murray entered the room and laid a file on the table in front of Neet. 'We've been doing background checks on O'Brien. Eleven years ago his best friend was killed. Cress Tyler. Twelve-year-old girl. It was a week before they found her body in an old mill. The coroner ruled it was an accident, but the Tyler family always suspected John was there when it happened and knew where she was all the time she was missing. They wanted him prosecuted but it was never proved.'

'Shit,' said Neet.

*

'Interview commences nine oh-seven.' Neet smoothed his hand over his face. He was tired. He wanted to sleep but he knew he wouldn't until the killer of Samantha Hedges was caught. He looked at John and tried to judge whether this was the man.

'John, who is Cress Tyler?'

The impact on John was instant. He started, sitting upright and staring at the door as though planning an escape. An expression of confused agitation overtook his face. Neet whistled. Bingo.

'John?' said Russell.

Lianne Carrington sat forward. 'This is a new line of enquiry. I wish to discuss it with my client before he makes any statement.'

Neet grinned. 'If you want,' he said. He nodded at John. 'If he wants...'

But John shook his head. 'Cress Tyler,' he said. 'She was my best friend. In school.'

'Girlfriend?'

'We were only twelve.'

'And?'

'She died.'

'You're a lucky guy to be around.'

John had regained his composure. He was sitting upright once more, staring at the detectives, his arms outstretched, palms upward. 'It was her. The accident. Not my brother. It was exactly as I described it, but it was Cress, not my brother.'

Neet groaned. 'So you told us the true and unexpurgated version of your childhood tragedy, except you somehow mistook your girlfriend for the brother you never had?'

'Yes.'

'For fuck's sake.' He slapped his hands on the desk in frustration. 'The thing is, John, this now links you to the sudden deaths of two twelve-year-old girls. And that changes everything.' He stopped and shook his head. ' Here's a question for you, because I'm sick of asking the other one. Did you kill Cress Tyler?'

John shot upright. 'No,' he said urgently. 'It was an accident.'

'You see, the difficulty we have, Detective Russell and I, is that once a lying bastard always a lying bastard. Do you see what I'm saying? Ever since you walked into this station you've been taking us for a ride. Is there a single word you've spoken, a single word, that is actually true?'

'I killed Samantha Hedges.'

'Forget Samantha Hedges. Let's concentrate on Cress Tyler. Did you kill Cress Tyler?'

'No.'

'Well, like I say, who can believe you, John? That's why I'm going to apply for an order to exhume her body.'

John jumped up, knocking his chair backwards against the wall. He looked around wildly and screamed, a high, piercing shriek that emanated from deep inside him. He paused for breath then screamed again, and again, and again. The detectives watched in horror as John convulsed in front of them, out of control, his body contorted like an animal in pain, still screaming, shrieking, yelling. He looked up and stared at Neet as though seeing him for the first time and lunged across the desk at him. Russell ran for the door and shouted for help as John took aim for Neet's throat with his hands. They fell together against the back wall and struggled for some moments, John scratching at Neet's face and neck.

Neet beat him away and swung him round and pulled his arm hard behind his back and pushed him hard against the wall. He struggled to catch his breath and braced himself for a further assault but John fell limp and leaned into the wall and pressed his face against it and started to cry. Logan and Murray rushed into the room and Murray handcuffed John and led him away. Russell and Neet stared at one another.

'Interview concluded nine eighteen,' said Neet. 'Ms Carrington, that man needs help. Make him talk to you.' Lianne Carrington, shocked into silence, nodded doubtfully.

The detectives decamped to their office. Russell slammed her files on the table. 'You never mentioned anything to me about an exhumation.'

'No. I just made it up on the spot. And you saw the impact it had on him ...'

'But what justification would we have? We have no evidence he did any harm to Cress Tyler. The coroner's report says it was an accident. No suspicious circumstances.'

'You saw how he reacted in there. He's got to be hiding something. You said so yourself. If we didn't have evidence before, that performance gives us reasonable doubt. You can't deny his behaviour is highly suspicious?'

'Everything about him is suspicious. That doesn't mean he's a murderer.'

'So exhume the body and find out.'

Russell shook her head. Eliminate the impossibles, isolate the improbables. It was highly improbable that Cress Tyler died as a result of foul play. It would have been investigated at the time. Forensics weren't so advanced eleven years ago, but they were still pretty efficient. If there was any indication of foul play it would have been on the record and it wasn't. Therefore, Cress probably died as a result of an accident. And the implication of that was clear: John didn't kill her. But, if John's description of the accident was true he must have come into contact with the body.

Next: it was highly improbable that John murdered Samantha Hedges because the DNA in the semen wasn't his. All the same, there was a minor DNA match which meant he had definitely come into contact with her. The big question, then, was whether Samantha was alive or dead when that happened? Alive: improbable, because she was in the hands of a murdering paedophile. Dead: therefore probable.

Was it impossible that he buried her? Or improbable? No, and no. So: a possible. John possibly buried the probably dead body of Samantha Hedges.

Two converging patterns. John did not cause the deaths of Cress Tyler and Samantha Hedges. But he knew about them.

She outlined her thinking to Neet. He looked unimpressed.

'The obvious question is why,' he said. 'I mean, if you come across the battered and mutilated body of a murdered child hidden in the undergrowth you don't tidy it away. What is he, a fucking Womble?'

'Because,' said Russell, suddenly weary, but the explanation forming in her head, 'because he didn't do right by Cress. He left her and she lay undiscovered for a week. Think how that would affect a twelve year old boy. He'd be seeing phantoms, zombies, whatever. Everywhere he turned he'd be seeing her, like Banquo's ghost come to haunt him. He's clearly still in trauma over it. That's something we can definitely agree on. He's completely rewritten it in his mind so that it wasn't even Cress who died. So what happens next? He's out walking and he discovers this body – dead body. What happens? His brain explodes. It's Cress. It's his little girlfriend. So what does he do? This is his chance. This time – finally – he does the right thing. To his way of thinking. He buries the body. Properly. Cress. The dead dead. Not walking dead.'

There was silence. 'You'd have to be one screwed-up mindfuck to think that,' said Neet.

'Well, that's one way to describe clinical psychosis. But don't you see? This whole thing is about getting rid of the guilt over Cress. It's tortured him all his adult life. He's never been able to escape her, or the memory, or the sense of failure. And now, now he finally manages to bury her. To say that she died without pain and that she's comfortably at rest. And what are you going to do? Dig her up again. Literally. You're going to exhume her body. No wonder he went fucking mental in there.'

Neet laughed.

'It's not funny.'

'It is actually. Tragic, I'll grant you, but definitely funny.' He laughed again and Russell watched with disgust. She walked out of the interview room and into the corridor. She stood outside the cell in which John O'Brien was being held for questioning about the murder of Samantha Hedges and the death of Cress Tyler. She opened the spy hole and looked at the forlorn body buried beneath a blanket. She wanted to connect, but there was no possibility.

Fresh Watter

The day I heard Jeannie was haein a bairnie I found a beezer of a pearl in the shallows of the Tay. It wid form a rare centre for the necklace I was makin but as I sat lookin at it that nicht, faither's words birlin in my ears, it fair lost its shine.

'Aye lookin like butter widnae melt in her mooth, the hoor,' faither said. 'Let that be a lesson tae you. Nivver trust the wenches.'

It was all I could do no tae cry but I'd hae got a hiding for that, so I dug my hen's claw intae my palm tae take my mind aff Jeannie Anderson. She was haein a bairnie. She'd been wi a man. It was a damned, damned shame.

There was a letter sittin on the table and I could see it was fae Geordie Tracey, the coalman. Faither wisnae a big reader and he was waitin for me tae tell him what it said. I stood in front of the windae tae get the light and read it oot. Faither was clatterin aboot wi the range like he wisnae really listenin but I kent fine he was. 'Dear Mr Kelty,' I read, 'I regret to inform you that you owe for three months coal and as a consequence I will not deliver any more until payment is made.'

'It's nearly summer onyway,' faither said.

It wasnae that near summer but I didnae argue. 'I'll speak tae the fairmer,' I said, 'and ask him if we can chop some wood.'

'Ye'll dae no such thing. And hae Andrew McAlister ken we're hard up? We'll manage.' He opened the range door and threw the letter intae the flames.

'Wee Boab', abody called me at school. Faither was near sixty and didnae let me mix wi other laddies. They werenae couth, he said. So I didnae hae ony friends. I was juist wee auld-fashioned Boab wi his funny words and short breeks and baggy jumper wi patches all ower it.

'It's no my fault,' I wanted tae tell them. 'I'm no that different fae you.' But wee Boab was the butt of abodies jokes. So I kept oot the way, went doon the Tay wi my glass-bottomed bucket and my rickety boat and floated on the watter lookin for pearls. Makin my necklace. A present for a lassie.

A lassie like Jeannie.

It was thinkin aboot Jeannie that got me intae trouble at school. We were only a wee school, thirty of us, all in one classroom. Jeannie was fifteen, twa years aulder than me, and she sat at the front, or at least she did until the bairnie. Noo her seat was empty, for the Dominie widnae let anyone else sit in it.

'Tarnished,' he said. 'Sullied. She's used goods now. Nobody will look at her again.' I mind his face when he said that, all stiff like he was needin a jobbie. I stared at her chair, imaginin her in it, her thin arms and long, dark hair, the way she curved, those lovely bosoms. I was in my ain wee world.

'Robert, what did I just say?' shouted the Dominie.

I had nae idea. It was somethin aboot thon Mr Churchill's Gold Standard that abody was fair vexed aboot. I'm sure it was awfae important but I couldnae see what it had tae dae wi us in Perthshire. The Dominie was standin ower my desk and I could smell the pipe smoke on his tweed suit. His nose was richt hairy. My heart started bangin and my haunds were shakin. I'd never got intae trouble wi the Dominie in my life.

'I'm awfae sorry, sir.'

'Next time I catch you not listening, Robert Kelty, it'll be six of the strap. Do you hear?'

'Aye sir.'

Abody else heard, too. I was black-affronted as they laughed at wee Boab gettin intae trouble.

Jeannie had her bairnie in March of 1927. 'That's the only thing the hussy's got richt,' said faither. 'All bairnies should be born in the springtime.'

'I was born in December,' I said and he clouted me that hard my lug was buzzin for half an hour. He mairched oot tae feed the cuddies and nae mair was said. Faither had nivver been a man tae laugh much, but since Christmas he'd been richt dowie.

It was a wee laddie Jeannie had, called Jimmy, and a handsome crater he was, too. She birled him aboot toon maist days in the black pram her mither bocht her in Perth. Abody smiled and cuddled the wee thing, and it seemed tae me that, apart fae the Dominie and faither, maist folks didnae seem tae mind awfae much aboot Jeannie and her bairnie.

She widnae say wha the faither was, juist smiled and said, 'Jimmy's precious, that's all that matters.' That made the Dominie worse. He forbade any mention of her name. 'Wickedness walks its own path, it needn't concern the righteous,' he said and placed a picter of oor lord Jesus Christ on her auld chair. I asked faither what for, and he said it was tae purify the air she breathed. She disnae breathe through her arse, I wanted tae say.

But it biled my insides that someone had done it wi Jeannie and I sair needed tae ken wha it was so's I could hate him. I tried hatin abody in toon, but that didnae satisfy. There was nae point in hatin Kenny the butcher – the man was eighty and blund, couldnae hae found his willie let alone use it. So I hated Jeannie instead, her and her bairn and the way she swaggered doon the street like she was a real wifie and no juist a fifteen-year-auld lassie lumbered wi a bairn afore her time.

I was countin the days till I could leave school and work on the fairm wi faither. Tending the heavy horses was a job for life, and I was guid at it already, which was mair than I could say for my schoolin. Whit did I want tae learn yon algebra for, or fancy English? I was fair stupit, I kent that, but I juist behaved mysel and was nae bother, no like the other laddies. Aye, but they all thocht it a grand wheeze tae try tae get me intae trouble. Ae time they left a deid puddock on Miss Massie's desk and blamed it on me. It didnae work, of course, for Miss Massie and the Dominie kent fine I wisnae the sort of laddie tae dae sic a thing.

But ae day they succeeded. Dauvit McTavish was makin a richt clatter at the back of the classroom while the Dominie was writin on the blackboard. The Dominie wisnae a man tae keep his temper lang and I was fell worried.

'Silence!' he shouted. Even though I hadnae done onything I was petrified. 'Any more noise and the whole class will get strapped.'

I kent I was done for. I could see them laughin and pointin at me.

'Wee Boabbie's goin tae get the belt,' Dauvit whispered tae me. I shook my heid, prayin they widnae dae sic a nasty thing.

Aye, but they did.

I think it was Andra McTavish wha farted, a topper that stunk like a rabbit deid in a ditch.

'That's it,' said the Dominie, throwin doon his chalk, ash-faced wi anger. He lined us up, the laddies and the lassies tae, and he strapped us fower times each. I was last and I was near greetin by the time it was my turn. Abody cheered. It hurt like stink.

But that was nothin. What wid faither say?

I sat on the side of the brae after school and checked my haunds tae see if there was ony bruisin. There wisnae, but faither would still ken. He'd see it on my face.

'Ye're lookin awfae worried, Bob.'

As if I didnae hae enough tae think aboot, it was Jeannie

Anderson. It wisnae that warm, but she was showin mair cleavage than Clara Bow, and I think she had lipstick on, too. Faither was richt aboot her, the hoor.

She spread her skirt oot and sat doon beside me, plonkin her bairnie on her knee. Funny, once upon a time I'd hae given all my pearls tae hae her sit next tae me, but noo I couldnae be fashed.

'Ach, I was juist wonderin whaur tae get some peewit eggs,' I said.

'As if you wouldn't know where tae get peewit eggs, you livin on a farm.' I felt mysel blush. It was like a warning – I couldnae lee tae save mysel. 'Would it be anythin to do with school that's botherin you?'

'Naw,' I said, ower fast.

'Bob!' She was teasing me, ticklin the bairn tae make it laugh as well. 'Dauvit told me what happened.'

'Well, hae a guid laugh. Abody else has.'

'I'm not laughin. But it's not that serious, is it? It doesn't matter. Abody gets the belt some time. Even wee Jimmy will, one day, won't you, ruffian?'

Silly lassie, bletherin tae her bairn as if bein a mither meant she knew the meanin of a'thing. She hadnae seen my faither in a temper. 'If you ever get intae trouble at school,' he'd say, 'I'll thrash ye twice as bad when ye get hame.'

So I put her richt, telt her faither would beat me black and blue.

'Well, don't tell him.'

'I cannae lee tae my faither.'

'It's not leein, you're just not telling him everything.'

'It's the same thing.'

'Course it's not. You don't tell everybody everything you do.'

'I do my faither, aye.'

'Oh, you've a lot to learn.'

Madam Muck, handin oot the words of wisdom. She

wisnae so wise ten months syne, when she was hoikin up her skirt for some cheap bastart that widnae stick by her.

'I'll tell you what,' she said, 'I'll come back with you. Explain to your father. It wasn't your fault.'

'No!' I shouted and I could see she was taken aback.

'Why not?'

I couldnae say that faither widnae let her within a mile of the fairm. If he knew I'd even been speakin tae her I'd get an even worse beatin. 'It's just my faither,' I said. 'He disnae like me talkin tae girls.'

Jeannie ruffled my hair. 'Bob Kelty, for someone who doesn't lie you tell a right lot of fibs.'

'An for someone who's sic a lot tae tell, you dinnae say awfae much.'

The moment I said it I was terrified. I looked away, like I could pretend I hadnae said it. I'm no one for confrontation. I aye lose. But Jeannie laughed.

'And what do you mean by that?'

I pointed tae the bairn. 'The faither.'

'Like I said, you don't tell everybody everything you do in life.'

I wanted tae argue, but how could I? I hadnae seen ony life.

'Aye well,' she said. 'I'll away home, Jimmy'll be needin his feed.' She cuddled the bairn tae her chest and its heid lolled tae one side. He watched me, his blue eyes all sparkly, juist like his mother's. The pair of them seemed awfae weel suited.

'What does he eat?' I said.

'What d'you think he eats? Why d'you think I've got these?' She shoogled her bosoms and my face burned hotter than a dung heap in August. I could hear her laughin as I ran doon the brae.

Faither was in a mood when I got hame. 'How was school?' he said. He nivver asked me about school. Nivver.

School was juist somethin tae be endured and it was of nae interest tae him or me. Why did he hae tae ask today of all days? I didnae answer and he scowled at me. He filled the kettle and stuck it on the range.

'Well?'

I had tae tell him. I kent what Jeannie said made sense but I couldnae dae it. 'I got intae trouble,' I said. 'It wisnae my fault. The whale class got the belt.'

'You got the belt?'

'Aye.'

'How mony?'

'Fower.'

He never said another word, juist walked oot tae the yard tae chop some kindlin. I kent that wisnae the end of it, though, and richt enough when he came back he stripped aff his belt and bent me ower the table and gied me eight strokes across the bahookie.

'I've telt you often enough,' he said, 'if you get intae trouble at school ye'll get it twice as bad fae me.'

He was shakin by the time he'd finished and I felt that guilty I apologised. 'I didnae mean tae disappoint you,' I said.

'We'll say nae mair,' he said but I could tell it was on his mind. He couldnae settle that evenin, up and doon, lookin in cupboards, bangin aboot. He took the shotgun oot of the wardrobe and started cleanin it, which was strange because that was a Sunday nicht job. And when he finished he left it lyin on the kitchen table, which was maist unusual, too, for he was generally richt particular aboot keepin it locked. I watched him quietly. He kept shakin his heid like he was arguin wi himsel. His haunds were shakin. I was sorry for bein sic a trial tae him but all the time I couldnae stop thinkin aboot Jeannie and her bairn. They seemed that happy thigither. The way the wee thing clung tae its mither was a sight tae behold.

Mostly, I nivver minded no' haein a mither. It seemed fae whit the other laddies said they spent maist of their time fussin ower you, and at least faither never did that. I'd nae memories of her, not one, and faither never spoke aboot her. In fact, there wisnae even a picter of her in the hoose.

Faither had a totty of whisky afore bedtime, which was maist unusual for a Friday, but I didnae mind. He was mair talkative when he'd had a nip and it was nice tae chat tae him man tae man. I dinnae ken what made me ask aboot mither that night – I didnae mean to, it just fell oot my gab.

Faither was silent. He poured himsel anither whisky and sat doon wi last week's *Sunday Post*, pretendin tae read it, but I kent he was goin tae speak. I could tell by the way his left leg was shooglin ower his right.

'Your mither's deid.'

'Aye, but how did she dee? And whit was she like? Was she bonny?' Noo that I'd started, I couldnae stop.

'Whit's past is past. Leave it.'

Maybe I was gettin fu' on the fumes of faither's whisky, or maybe I didnae think I'd get twa beatins in one day, but I kept on at him, long efter I should have stopped.

'Enough!' he shouted. I shrank back in my chair. He could turn awfae fast and when he did you didnae hing aboot. But I was flabbergasted by what happened next.

He started greetin.

My faither. Greetin. I didnae ken whaur tae look. The man was aside himsel, his haunds gripped roond his knees, his heid doon and his body all rigid except for his chest, which was heavin like he'd juist raced Eric Liddell in the hundred yards. I went tae bed no tae embarrass him further.

When I came ben for breakfast the next mornin he was pokin aboot in the cupboards again. I didnae hear him come tae bed and he looked like he hadnae slept. There were bills and papers all ower the table. Finally he let oot a cry and came up wi an auld, tattered envelope.

'Does that say General Accident?' he said.

'Aye.'

He left it on the sideboard and went oot tae chop wood. When I was sure he was gone I had a look. It was a life insurance policy for fifty pounds and I supposed he was goin tae cash it in tae pay the coalman. That was good, onyway. He came back and drapped an armful of logs on the stane floor.

'Ye're goin tae hae tae grow up,' he said.

I was fell upset he was still disappointed in me for gettin the belt. 'Aye,' I said. 'Sorry.'

When I finished my chores I went doon the river tae look for pearls. I'd been there maybe an hour when I saw Jeannie by the watterside.

'Hello,' she said. 'I didn't see you there, with yer head in that bucket.'

'Best way tae find pearls.'

'Aye? And who would you be collecting pearls for?'

I turned the boat tae shore and I dinnae think she noticed me blushin. We sat by the riverbank and I explained all aboot the pearl fishin. It's no complicated but she seemed fair impressed. Aye, but she was easy company. I'm no awfae sure wi people, bein a bit of a dunderheid, but Jeannie was a couthy lass and she made me feel braw.

'Why do you keep looking over my shoulder?' she said, laughin. 'Are you worried somebody might see us together?'

I tried tae deny it but she laughed even more.

'My faither,' I heard mysel sayin. The truth juist falls oot my mooth sometimes.

'Your faither? Does he not approve of me?'

'Naw.' There was nae point denying it.

'Well let me tell you, Bob Kelty, wee Jimmy's the best thing that's ever happened to me. I look into his eyes and what do I see? I hold him and what do I feel? I dream about him. I wake up in the morning and rush to his cot to look at him. Just look at him. I feel him all cosy against me, his wee hand curled against mine. Eyes staring into mine. And I see what he's thinking. It's plain on his face. He's thinking I'm his mother and he loves me. Isn't that the most special thing you could ever imagine?'

Jeannie's eyes were shiny wi tears. Jings, first faither, noo her.

'Dinnae you start,' I said.

'Start what?'

'Greetin.'

'Why? Who else has been greetin?' Suddenly, she became the bossy besom again and I was juist wee Boab and she widnae let up. 'Who else has been greetin on you? Tell me. Tell me.'

In the end, I gave in. 'Faither,' I said.

'Your faither!'

'Wheesht.'

'Your father was greetin? Why?'

I found mysel explainin a'thing, aboot my mither, how he wouldnae talk aboot her. How much I wanted tae ken aboot her. It was a fell relief, for I'd been thinkin aboot it all morning.

'The poor man,' she said.

I was amazed. I was expectin sympathy for me, no him. 'Come aff it,' I said.

'What?'

'Jings, the man's juist like you. There's you, winnae say onythin aboot the faither of that bairn. And there's faither, winnae speak a word aboot my mither. Whit's the difference? Ye cannae say 'poor man' aboot him when ye're daein the same thing yersel.'

She smiled. 'Aye, maybe. But there's a right time and a wrong time for telling, and a right reason and a wrong one. I'll probably never speak about it, and I have my reasons. But I'm not your father, I can't speak for him.'

'I tell ye, it's ower complicated, this growin up. Sometimes ye should, sometimes ye shouldnae. Wha's tae ken?'

Jeannie smiled. Jimmy started tae greet and she draped him ower her chest and patted his back.

'He'll be needin a feed,' I said.

'Aye, I'd best be off home.'

She looked smashin. She seemed tae glow wi the mitherhood. 'You could do it here,' I said. 'There's naebody aboot.'

'Except you.'

'Och, I widnae mind.'

'Would ye not?'

I didnae ken what I was feelin, juist then. It was like I was goin tae be sick. There were too many thochts in my heid for my stupit brain tae manage. I wanted tae ken aboot my mither but I'd nae way of findin oot. I thocht aboot faither, greetin intae his whisky. I thocht about the Dominie, plonkin a picter of Jesus Christ on Jeannie's chair. Callin her 'used goods'. Well, it seemed tae me Jeannie and her bairnie were juist grand. I could see their love. Feel it.

I wanted it.

'No, Jeannie,' I said. 'It's no right tae hide things.'

She smiled. She nodded and began to unbutton her blouse. It was the maist beautiful thing I ever saw.

As I walked hame afterwards wi my bucket empty and my heid fu, I thocht aboot faither tellin me I'd hae tae grow up. Well, I thocht, I wisnae a wee laddie any more now.

Aye, so's I thocht.

The door was locked when I got hame. It was never locked. I didnae hae a key. I walked roond the back and keeked in the kitchen windae.

'Faither?' I shouted.

But I kent already faither wasnae goin tae answer.

The Entertainer

Carmela Cant bowled into the living room and slapped her sister on the back of the head and launched herself onto the piano stool.

'Alright shrimp?' she said in a Donald Duck voice.

'I was until you hit me.'

'I'm toughening you up. It's a hard world out there.'

'It's a hard world in here.'

Carmela opened the piano lid and rested her fingers on the keys. She turned and bared her teeth in an exaggerated grimace.

'Showtime,' she quacked.

She faced the piano and played the opening notes of *The Entertainer*. It was the only tune she knew, although she didn't know it very well. The slow and melodic introduction was easy and the first section was so familiar she could play it without thinking but, when the tune shifted to the second phase, her rhythm began to crumble. She slowed to a crawl, crouching over the piano and working out the fingering as she went. Then, when she reached the main melody again, she speeded to a gallop as though trying to make up for lost time. The tune weaved in and out of its time signature. Three bars in the middle were in waltz time, Carmela's body swaying with the music. Behind her, Maria did likewise, laughing, waving her hands in the air. Carmela ran through the tune three times and each time the same idiosyncrasies were manifested at the same moments, as though this were how it should be played. Trot, falter, gallop, falter, waltz. By the time both Carmela and tune staggered to a conclusion it was closer to freeform jazz, a sweating, roaring, staggering drunkard of a performance, so wrong it was magnificent. On the final bar she sang tunelessly and lustily, 'The entertainer is star, the entertainer is star, the entertainer is star of the show. Boom boom.'

She bounced off the piano, singing the line over and over, cackling, pulling her face into a demented grin, all teeth and gums, and skipped past her sister to the door.

'Come on, shrimp, the Entertainer will buy you an ice cream.' She was gone before Maria could react and out of the house before she could get her coat and halfway up Church Street before she was at the garden gate. By the time Maria caught her up at Crolla's, Carmela had eaten half her ice cream and was holding Maria's impatiently. She was fifteen, looked eighteen, acted ten.

Maria took the ice cream and licked it greedily, happy in the company of her sister. Maria was the quiet one, two years younger and identical to Carmela in appearance but not nature. Where Carmela was dramatic Maria was reserved, content to remain in the shadows. At home, she played the willing audience, quiet conspirator, giggler beneath the bedsheets when Carmela riled their mother at lights out by harumphing down the stairs like Donald Duck. Outside the home, though, the reverse was true, Maria gregarious and settled in school while Carmela was reserved and diffident with her peers. Maria saw this dichotomy, saw Carmela constantly alone in the playground, saw the wall of reticence around her, but thought nothing of it. That was Carmela. She danced to her own beat. Carmela, meanwhile, looked inward.

'Look,' said Maria, pointing towards the cinema, 'it's your boyfriend.'

Carmela scowled. 'Stop it.'

The great romance between Carmela and Kenny McAskill

had been invented by Maria last Christmas and the more it annoyed Carmela the more Maria persisted with the rumour, elaborating, inventing rendezvous, ticking down the days until they would declare an inevitable engagement.

'Hi, Kenny,' she said as the young boy passed.

'Hiya.' He looked from Maria to Carmela. 'Hi Carmela,' he said.

'Hi Kenny,' Carmela shouted as Donald Duck. 'How'sh it going?' Kenny gave her a mystified look and walked past and Carmela watched him go. She saw Maria staring at her.

'What?' she said.

'You spoke to him like Donald Duck.'

'No, I didn't.'

'Yes, you did. That's why he walked away.'

'Waaaggghhh.'

*

The rendition of *The Entertainer* the next evening was even more manic than normal. Carmela thundered the piano keys as though at war with them. She played the tune over and over, seven or eight times, ever faster, ever louder. Alongside, she wailed a Donald Duck accompaniment, screeching the words until the whole room seemed to be engulfed by her noise. 'The Entertainer ish shtar of the show,' she screeched, then stood up and stormed to the door.

'Pity the show's shite,' she shouted and slammed the door behind her. The piano was still ringing a minute later. So were Maria's ears.

'What's up with her?' Maria's mother stood in the doorway, dish towel in her hand. Maria shrugged.

'She's been like it since she got home.'

Later, Maria would reflect that Carmela's silence for the remainder of that evening was the first of many to follow. Over the coming months, they would arrive more frequently and last longer, but this first time no one thought much of it. Maria studied her sister, the resolute blankness, total detachment. Her face seemed to have been fixed into some kind of invisible mask. It gave the appearance of her sister but it was as though she wasn't there, as though she were inhabiting two dimensions only.

'You alright?' Maria said when they were in bed.

Carmela turned off the light and lay on her back. 'I got the belt.'

'Who from?'

'Mr Stutz.'

'Latin? But that's your favourite subject.'

'Don't tell Mum.'

'Of course not.' Maria stared into the gradually unfolding shape of the darkness, watching the outlines of their furniture emerge as though being created afresh in a charcoal drawing. 'What happened?' she said.

'It was Latin declension. It was my turn. Second declension nouns.'

'Yeah?'

'I did it as Donald Duck.' She turned towards her sister. 'Shervus, shervum, shervi, shervo, shervo.'

Maria laughed. 'You didn't?'

'Shervi, shervos, shervorum, shervis, shervis.'

Maria laughed again and shushed herself, looking at their closed bedroom door with alarm.

'It would have been alright,' said Carmela. 'Mr Stutz was even laughing. But then I jumped up and went 'waaaggghhh' in his face at the end. That did it.'

'Ha! Was he really mad?'

'Quit laughing. It's not funny.'

'It's only the belt.'

'You don't get it. That pain, it's inside me now. It'll never go away.'

'What do you mean?'

Maria waited. She wanted Donald Duck to blow her a

raspberry and say 'Goodnight Shrimp', but nothing more was said and eventually she turned round and lay facing the door and thought about her sister.

*

The following morning Carmela appeared refreshed. She smiled at her sister and joked and they talked about going to Perth at the weekend to buy records. The calm didn't last. Maria heard at playtime that Carmela had been in trouble again and had been sent to the rector's office. She waited for her at lunchtime but there was no sign. Nor at afternoon playtime. At twenty to four she saw her turning right out of school and heading for Duchlage Road. She hurried after.

'Carmela.'

Carmela turned. Her face was rigid, emotionless. 'Fuck off,' she yelled in Donald Duck. 'Leave me alone. Waaaggghhh.'

For two weeks Carmela spoke only as Donald. At school she said nothing, tried to disappear, tried not to impinge on its daily routines. Through seeking to become invisible she became the centre of attention and three lunchtimes in succession Maria had to take her hand and walk her along the deserted railway line at the back of the playing fields and talk to her and soothe her and calm her down.

'Please come back to me,' she said.

'I can't,' said Donald.

'Why not?'

'I don't know who I am.'

'Don't talk daft.'

Carmela started to cry. At first they were only gentle sobs but almost immediately they overtook her whole body as if, once released, the emotion was unstoppable. She shuddered and heaved, bending low over the stones of the old railway line, wailing in pain. There was an abandoned sofa at the edge of the track and Maria steered her sister into it and knelt beside her and took her hand. Carmela let out a loud Donald caterwaul.

'Please, Mellie, stop with the Donald Duck. It's not funny anymore.'

'It never was funny,' said Donald. Carmela stared at the sky, her jaw clenched, and would say no more. After a few minutes Maria wasn't even sure whether her sister knew she was still beside her. When she took her hand and walked her back to school it was like leading an inanimate object.

Maria debated later whether or not to tell her mother. It had always been the Cant girls against the world, and especially against the Cant parents. To talk about Carmela behind her back would feel like a betrayal.

'Please don't tell her I said anything,' she told her mother afterwards. Isobel Cant turned away and faced the cooker, stirring a pot that didn't need stirring. The evening was difficult. Nobody spoke. The argument waited to happen.

'How was your day?' her mother asked.

'Okay,' said Donald.

'Enough!' Isobel Cant stood in front of Carmela. 'Stop speaking in that stupid voice. From this moment on it's forbidden. Is that clear?'

Carmela stared at her. Silently, she drew a zip across her mouth. She stood up and walked out of the room and went to her bed. When Maria joined her at bedtime she turned to face the wall and rested her head on her hands and closed her eyes and didn't even open them when she heard Maria sobbing.

The next morning she would not speak and Donald Duck gave way to Marcel Marceau. At breakfast she mimed spreading butter on her hand and Maria passed her the butter dish. She mimed pouring from a teapot and her mother filled her cup.

'You can speak,' Isobel Cant said. 'Just not in that voice.'

Carmela tilted her head and gave a sad smile, her eyes

wide and staring. She mimed tears falling down her cheek and shrugged her shoulders and spread her arms, palms upwards, in a gesture of supplication. And she mimed, once more, a zip being drawn across her mouth. Then she gave a slow wave and retreated backwards from the room and walked to school on her own with her hood up.

Her existence became a void of silence. At school she developed hiding mechanisms. In class, it was best to sit in the front rows, invisible in full sight. Be attentive but not too attentive, just enough to convince the teacher she was listening. At the bell she knew to be either first or last out or the classroom. The playground was impossible but she found if she went to the very end of the smokers' wall beside the hockey pitches she could be on her own. None of her classmates would walk past the smokers, fourth and fifth years who cultivated an air of menace. Nobody else came near. If she kept her back to the smokers and ignored their occasional shouts she could be isolated in her own dominion.

'Hello.'

She turned round in irritation, her hands buried deep in her blazer pockets, cigarette hanging from her mouth. It was Friday lunchtime and she had negotiated the whole week without speaking. Two more hours and she could retreat to the safety of home and spend two days without having to avoid anyone or disappear or brood.

'How are you?' Kenny McAskill gave her a nervous smile. Carmela frowned. Kenny was another of the school weirdos like her, a boy two years below who rarely spoke and had few friends. Everyone thought he was thick. He looked at her expectantly.

'Uuuggghhh,' she said, pulling a face. She turned away in order not to see the harm she had done, and when she looked back he had gone. She immediately regretted her actions. She looked around, at the empty playing fields stretching into the distance, the railway line beyond, the flatness of the arable valley. In the distance the Ochils stood in a circle around the town. They were like a wall, enclosing her in her own private hell.

*

After two weeks she broke her silence. When Maria came home from choir practice after school she heard *The Entertainer* being played in the front room. She smiled and looked at her mother in the kitchen. Isobel Cant shrugged.

'She just came in, said "Hi Mum" like nothing was different and went through there and started playing the piano.'

Maria went into the living room and flopped onto the settee and watched and listened. Carmela was bouncing about on the piano stool as though she was living every note. Her hands flew exaggeratedly across the keys. She turned and gave an enormous grin and began to sing, high and tunelessly. When she had played *The Entertainer* six times she stopped with a final flourish.

'I'm the entertainer, me. I can dance and sing, I can do most anything. Feed me, want me, wind me up. Watch the show me show me show.'

'Welcome back,' said Maria.

'Have you been away?' She gave a Donald Duck cackle and turned and played *The Entertainer* again, slower than slow. It was oddly beautiful. 'The entertainer is star, the entertainer is star, the entertainer is star of the show.'

'And what a show it is,' said Maria.

In the coming months there followed a cycle of muteness and mania. Two weeks of euphoric energy would be followed by weeks of silence, noise into sullenness, laughter to anger. Carmela's wild moments grew wilder. She broke her ankle jumping down the stairs the week before Christmas. Through it all, she became increasingly introspective and the periods of silence grew progressively longer. They always ended with her playing *The Entertainer*. Maria tried to understand what triggered the changes but they seemed entirely random. Only Carmela could know, and she wouldn't say.

In the periods of silence the sisters learned to communicate through gestures and intuition. Carmela would raise an eyebrow as if to ask 'okay shrimp?' and Maria would smile and nod. If Maria mimed playing the piano she could gauge from Carmela's response how far she was from a return to activity. Their mutual disdain for their parents was acted out in lengthy and detailed and profound performances. In this way Maria convinced herself everything remained normal, while Carmela retained some connection with reality. She grew to enjoy the feeling of disconnection. There was so much agglomerated pain inside her, accumulated over years of unhappiness and disappointment, that silence became a desirable ache, a beautiful surface to her terrible depth. Slowly, during these periods, the tensions in her mind eased. She could concentrate. She could plan. She could dream.

I'm the entertainer
In silence I sing
I dance through the pain
I punish my brain
I laugh at the sane
Throw love down the drain
The entertainer is me
Entertainment I am
The entertainer is me
Entertainment I can.

'Why do you do it?' Maria asked during one of Carmela's speaking periods. They sat on the bank of the reservoir on the Knock. An eastern wind buffeted them and they huddled into their jackets and sat close together, knees touching. The position of the sun created only one shadow for the pair of them, emanating from Carmela's feet.

'I don't do anything.'

'You do. You don't speak to anyone.'

'So that's not doing anything.'

'But why?'

The surface of the reservoir shivered, pulsing in the wind as though a current was bearing it west. 'Sometimes I feel that everything inside my brain is going to explode. The pain gets too much...'

'What pain?'

'Everything pain. Every pain I've ever felt is still inside me. Every nasty thing anyone's said to me. Every bad thing I've ever done. Every moment of hate, fear, boredom, sadness. Nothing goes away. It just keeps building. Getting worse.'

'And silence is your way of managing it?'

Carmela stared at her fingers. She turned her hands round and stared at her palms. She gripped her hands into fists. 'It's not like that. Not as neat as that. It's not a conscious decision. It just happens. I can't control it.'

'But it helps?'

'Nothing helps. But it delays.'

'Delays what?'

Carmela shook her head. She looked out at the barren reservoir. 'I don't know.'

*

In May, Maria was called to the rector's office and made to wait outside for ten minutes. By the time she was shown inside she was in a state of terror. She had never seen the rector closer than from the stage at Monday assembly. He sat opposite her and flashed a smile. His breath smelled.

'How's your sister?'

'Fine.'

'Really?'

'Yes.'

'Only her behaviour is somewhat erratic. I'm sure you've noticed. I'm sure you're worried about it. I know we are.'

'Carmela just keeps herself to herself.'

'Does she have problems at home?'

'No.'

'Are you sure?'

Maria stared at him and retreated into silence. Sisters together. Nobody else understood Carmela and it was up to Maria to protect her.

'Has Carmela ever talked about harming herself?'

Maria sat back as though she had been stung. 'No,' she said firmly. 'She wouldn't do that.'

The rector nodded and thanked her and said she could go. She retreated with relief and opened the door. Outside, on the same seat she had occupied half an hour before, Carmela was waiting. She looked up at her younger sister and closed her eyes for three or four seconds. When she opened them Maria drew a zip over her mouth. Carmela stared at her for some moments then shook her head. She pulled a zip across her own mouth in the opposite direction and immediately opened her mouth wide and gave a silent scream.

'No,' said Maria but Carmela's eyes were closed again and they would not open until Maria had gone.

By the time she was shown through to the rector's office, quarter of an hour later, Carmela had retreated further inside herself than she had ever explored. The pain was physical and mental at once, pouring through every vein and sinew and bone. It occupied her entirety. She tried to concentrate but it was impossible. Every thought trailed to Maria. Every thought ached. She sat before the rector and closed her eyes and lowered her head and clasped her hands tightly in her lap. His voice was low and sinuous as a snake.

'Maria is very concerned about you.'

Maria would never betray me.

'We're all concerned, Carmela.'

Maria would never betray me.
'How are things at home?'
Maria would never betray me.
'Maria suggested that perhaps things were difficult at home?'
Maria.
'She's worried, Carmela. She's worried that you might harm yourself. Have you ever had thoughts like that?'
Maria.
'We want to work with you, Carmela. Offer support. A professional. Would you like that?'
I'm the entertainer.
'However, that will take some time. We know your schoolwork is already suffering. You're very clever. You should be getting straight As. You still can.'
It's the show me show me show me show.
'For that reason we want you to stay back in Third Year next year. We don't think you're quite ready for your O Grades yet. Another year, with support from the psychologist, you'll be right as rain. What do you say?'
Where do shadows go when the sun disappears?

*

When Maria walked out of the High School that evening after choir practice she could see and hear, up the hill and across the field, a gathering on Maxtone Road, close to her house. She felt a heavy sickness in her stomach and started to run. At the five roads some acquaintances, older girls, passed her, sniggering.

'Best get home,' said Shona McMorran. It was like a punch to the stomach, confirmation of trouble. Carmela, she thought, please be okay.

A crowd of forty or fifty had gathered outside the house, laughing and braying. It sounded coarse, an exercise in communal cruelty. Maria recognised school friends and neighbours, people she had thought kind, people she would now never trust again. The Galvin twins, so-called friends of Carmela, Andrea Prest, Helen Lewis and her mum. Others. The crowd parted to let her through and in the hush Maria could hear *The Entertainer*. It was too loud to be coming from inside the house.

'Oh Carmela.'

The piano was wedged in the front door, stuck half in and half out, teetering on the doorstep. Carmela was naked and her face was painted like a Pierrot. She was playing *The Entertainer* with her left hand and those notes she could reach with her right hand before the doorframe blocked her way. The notes she couldn't reach she sang. Each time she pressed hard on the bottom keys the piano tilted downwards into the void above the doorstep and she had to depress a clutch of higher notes to bring it level again. She was oblivious of the crowd behind her, focused only on the piano and her pain and the intimate present.

'It's the show me show me show me show,' she yelled as Donald Duck. 'The show me show me show me show. I'm the entertainer. The entertainer is shtar, the entertainer is shtar, the entertainer is shtar of the show...'

Maria took off her coat and draped it across Carmela's shoulders. Carmela carried on playing, giving no indication she was even aware of her sister's presence. Maria took her arm.

'Oh, you're so cold,' she said. She put her arm around her and rested her head against her shoulder. She clasped her hand and gripped it tightly. Carmela's mouth was moving, her features in constant agitation, as though she were embroiled in an argument entirely of her own. She was not in this reality, and Maria regretted pulling her back into it. Maybe she was better where she was. 'Come on,' she said.

Carmela pointed to the ground, to her shadow on the path formed by the late springtime sun.

'I'm not the entertainer,' she said. 'I'm the entertainer's shadow.'

'You are the entertainer. You always will be. But sometimes can't you just be Carmela? My favourite big sister.'

'Do you love me?'

'Courshe I love you,' Maria quacked.

'That wash pathetic.'

'I know. So teach me?'

'Waaaggghhh.'

'Waaaggghhh.'

A Curious Judgement

The facts were these: John Caw, a man weel-kent to possess a pushionous nature, stole three sheep from George Buchan's flock grazing on feu land at Ferntower. He did not deny the charge and the sheep were found outside his howff on the edge of Monzie. He would surely hang. Edward Morrison, seated in the snug of the Clansman Tavern, sipped his sherry.

'If he could only have curbed his appetite a few months longer, until the Capital Crimes Bill becomes law, his neck would surely have been saved.'

Archibald Neil grimaced. 'That bill will be the most egregious error ever committed by parliament. Servants and workers will have nothing to fear if the capital deterrent is removed for all manner of offences. Every gentleman in the country will see his household riven by breaches of trust. Every business owner will be confronted by disputatious staff. We will be bound for anarchy, mark you.'

'The capital deterrent did nothing to restrain John Caw.'

'John Caw is a degenerate. The law cannot save such people. It serves only to save us from them.' He lit a cheroot and threw the lucifer into an ashtray. 'But who will save us from those deuced reformers in parliament with their reckless notions?'

'You can't deny reform is required?'

'Why? Are we not managing perfectly well? The country is prosperous. Our streets are safe. Scoundrels like John Caw will face the force of the law and be marched to the scaffold.'

Morrison raised his schooner to his lips once more. 'I will surely lose in court tomorrow, and when I do I won't shed a tear for John Caw. But the lad... I would not see him hang.'

'I don't believe the boy will hang. He was forced against his will.'

'You will say that in court?'

'Of course not. I'm acting for the prosecution. Why should I do your work for you?'

'But you will not protest too loudly?'

'My intention is for John Caw to hang. If that is the outcome I will be satisfied.'

*

The gallery of the High Court of Justiciary on the Royal Mile was full, the prospect of a double murder conviction attracting idle observers from across the city. Mr Morrison rose and addressed the boy in the dock.

'Peter McCausland, you admit you aided John Caw with his malign activities?'

'His whit?'

'Stealing sheep.'

'Aye.' A murmur ran round the court and Judge Hamilton shouted for silence. McCausland looked up at the gallery as though aware for the first time of their presence. He nodded at his mother and she gave a tight, frightened smile in return. He was a tall lad of sixteen, pleasant-featured but a sallow complexion evidence of his confinement in Perth Prison this past month. His voice was firm but halting.

'Explain to me the circumstances,' said Morrison.

'I was walkin past Ferntower, to my work at Milnab Mill, and John Caw shouted to me to help him.'

'Help him steal sheep?'

'Aye.'

'And what did you do?'

'I said no.'

'Why?'

'Sheep stealin. It's against the law.'

'And you don't break the law?'

'No. My mither would clap my lug.' He looked up at her again as laughter rang round the court.

'And yet you did it. Why?'

McCausland gestured to the man seated in the dock, John Caw. He was short and barrel-chested, clearly muscular beneath a worn and threadbare jacket and collarless shirt. He stared at McCausland with contempt.

'He said he'd knap me ower the heid if I didnae help him.'

'Assault you?'

'Aye. Do me in, ken?'

'Let me be clear. You believed your life might be in danger if you didn't help Mr Caw?'

'Aye.'

'No further questions.'

Mr Neil rose wearily, his knees creaking, the breakfast kippers sitting uneasily in his stomach. He limped to the dais. 'You know sheep stealing to be a capital crime?'

'Aye.'

'And yet you chose to embark on this nefarious endeavour?'

'He threatened me.'

Neil turned to face John Caw in the dock. He waved his arm dismissively. 'Mr Caw,' he said, 'is certainly a powerful-looking man. I should not like to encounter him alone after dark. However, he does not strike me as fleet of foot.'

'Eh?'

'Surely a fit and healthy young man like you could have outrun him?'

'I could hae outrun him then, aye.'

'Then why didn't you?'

'How lang d'you want me to keep runnin?'

'Until you had effected your escape.'

'And whit aboot the next day? Or the day efter? Or the day efter?'

'You seriously suppose you would be the subject of a sustained vendetta by Mr Caw?'

'I believe he'd do me in.'

Neil turned to the jury. 'Fanciful nonsense. We're talking about Crieff here. A quiet town in rural Perthshire. It's hardly Border Reiver territory.' Neil was gratified to see smiles break out on the faces of most of the jurors. They seemed a malleable lot. He thought to continue but realised his point was made.

'No further questions.'

Morrison replaced him once more at the dais, irritated that Neil, after suggesting he had no interest in proving McCausland's complicity, should now be attempting to do exactly that.

'When you say you "believe he'd do me in", do you have just cause for such supposition?' He caught the look of confusion on McCausland's face. 'Why did you think that?' he explained.

'He put Jamesie McAllister in the hospital last month. Broken skull. And Archie Cram, the man's half-daft noo. Gibbers and slavers aw wey.'

'As the result of an attack by Mr Caw?'

'His ain mither didnae recognise him when she fund him.'

Morrison paused for a moment to give the jury time to reflect on this evidence. As one, they were staring at Caw. Their animosity was evident. That was good. He faced them.

'What would you have done?' he asked. He pointed at McCausland and then at Caw. 'These two men, it is obvious, are entirely different in character. Caw admits what he did. He's a man of violence, a ruffian with a long criminal record, coming from a criminal family. His father is proud to boast that he was the last man to be held in the Crieff town stocks. But Peter McCausland, he's a mill lad, from a good family. His mother's here today, and look at the worry on her face. Peter McCausland is cut from a different cloth. The poor lad was simply in the wrong place at the wrong time. That could have been you.'

*

'Nicely summed up.' Neil puffed on his cheroot in the snug of the Clansman. 'Played to their emotions. An innocent laddie, out of his depth.'

'I should not have required the effort,' replied Morrison, still in high dudgeon regarding Neil's behaviour, 'had you not essayed a character assassination of the lad first.'

'Nonsense, man. I had to say something of the sort. The jury had to be won round by the weight of your argument. The power of your rhetoric. You needed something to argue against. I provided that.'

Morrison pointed his finger at him. 'Perhaps your "provision" was over-generous.'

'Not at all. I could have made the jury believe much worse of your young man, had I been so inclined. As it is, your response was adequate."

Adequate. Morrison knew that theirs was a profession in which "adequate" was seldom sufficient. 'You think I've done enough?'

'All that's required now is for Judge Hamilton to see sense. Death for Caw, life for McCausland.'

'But will he do so?'

'I see no reason why not. You can be thankful it's Judge Hamilton, not Judge Thomson. Harold Thomson would hang the pair of them without waiting for the formality of a jury's decision.'

'And me too, for the impertinence of trying to defend them.'

'Precisely. Whereas Fraser Hamilton is a man not given to excesses. I had lunch with him in Saville's last month and apart from fulminating at length against this deuced bill, he was quiet in the extreme. Only ate three courses. Barely a quart of port afterwards.'

*

Judge Hamilton addressed the jury, his hands clasped in front of him as though in supplication. 'You have found both Caw and McCausland guilty of sheep stealing and it now falls to me to pass sentence. This is a distressing case, occurring at a distressing time. Our politicians in Westminster are interfering with the law, sticking their noses where they assuredly do not belong. I greatly deprecate the bill going through parliament as we speak, reducing the number and nature of capital offences. Soon, little more than murder and high treason will be punishable by death and this country will reap a bitter harvest of disharmony and dishonour. Criminals will be released from concern for their own mortality. They will be emboldened. Crime will become endemic. This is a foolishness we will all live to regret.

'Turning to this case, in the matter of John Caw there is but one sentence available.' He took the black cap proffered by the usher and placed it on his wig. 'John Caw, the sentence of the court upon you is that you be taken from this place to a lawful prison and thence to a place of execution and that you be hanged by the neck until you are dead; and that your body be afterwards buried within the precincts of the prison in which you shall be confined before your execution. And may the Lord have mercy on your soul. Amen.'

Caw shook his head and made to stand but a militiaman restrained him. Peter McCausland, separated from Caw by a second militiaman, looked to his mother in the gallery. Morrison watched on, fear rising in his throat. Judge Hamilton turned to McCausland.

'As to the case of the accomplice – for that is what he was, an accomplice – there is a decision to be made. Assuredly, there was a degree of coercion involved. I can imagine Caw to be a brute of a man best not argued with. Nonetheless, this young boy has allowed himself to behave in a heinous fashion. There is therefore the likelihood that a bad habit has been formed.' He looked up at the jury.

'I am of the belief that, to prevent subsequent danger from this young man, a capital sentence must also be handed down.'

A wail arose from the gallery, resounding around the courtroom. Peter McCausland's mother rose to her feet, fisted hands waving helplessly in the air. 'No,' she screamed. 'No, no, no.' She looked to her son, mouth agape, an expression of horror etched on her world-wearied features. Peter gave her a weak smile, pathetic, pitiful, and she stopped screaming, mouth still open and eyes staring. Then she turned her gaze and fixed it on Edward Morrison. Those eyes, those eyes filled with hatred, terror, outrage.

Hopelessness. The nihilism of the oppressed.

Morrison and Mrs McCausland stared at one another in silence. And then she screamed again, screamed until there was no more breath in her lungs. And, when she had recharged them, she screamed again.

*

'A most curious judgement,' Neil said afterwards, back in the snug of the Clansman. 'It would have been a fitting sequel to have hanged the sheep also, since they allowed themselves to be driven away by those who had no right to do so.'

'Give it time,' said Morrison. 'The law may get there eventually.'

'I confess, I did not foresee such a sentence from Fraser Hamilton.'

'It is a calumny. That young man has been sentenced to

death, not because of his own actions, but because of the actions of six-hundred-and-fifty men four hundred miles away.'

'And because a judge is angry that his opportunities to pass a sentence of death will be greatly reduced.'

Morrison's sherry remained untouched before him. He ground his jaw and stared fixedly ahead. 'You say that, yet the words he used and the sentiments he expressed were almost the same as those you gave to me in this very room two days ago.'

Neil reflected. 'It is true, in my opinion, that the criminal classes will have more to celebrate from the Capital Crimes Act than the honest man. But not all criminals are degenerates. Young McCausland demonstrates that. He does not deserve his fate.'

'The system has conspired to seal it.'

There was a pause, then Neil spoke slowly. There was a tiredness in his voice, an unwonted hesitancy. 'There is, perhaps, a need for wider reforms after all.'

Morrison closed his eyes. He could hear still the howl of terror from the wretch McCausland's mother. That was a sound he knew he would never forget. Nor those eyes. Not ever.

'Alas, too late for Peter McCausland,' he said.

'Too late,' said Neil.

Brainspotting

Choose truth. Choose beauty. Choose morality, reason, choose history. Choose humanity. Choose tae examine in exquisite detail the ultimate questions aboot the nature ay reality, the meaning ay life. Choose questions. Choose debate an logic an the full flourish ay the human mind.

Choose tae extend an argument just that wee bit too far an make an arse ay yersel. Choose tae argue the toss wi every fucker who walks through the door ay the Star an Garter an convince him that nothin, least ay aw him, is, in fact, real. Choose tae get yer heid panned in. Choose misery.

Choose philosophy.

Saturday morning, eight am, fuckin insomniac city. Anither day ay this pishin torment, ma brain screamin for philosophy. Jist a wee skoosh wis aw ah needed tae see me through. Ah wis goin ootma skull wi the lack ay words. Felt like the ones ah had were crawling ootma every orifice an if ah didnae get a fix real soon ah'd be a clunkheid like awbody else in this fuckin Leith hellhole. Me, Jean-Jacques Rousseau, man ay science an philosophy, deid twa hundert year, reduced tae this.

Ah tried tae calm masel wi memories ay ma glorious Mme de Warens, the one love ay ma sorry life, but aw thae lost opportunities came back tae me and, onyhow, slushy reminiscence wasnae the philosopher's way. Readin! Writin! Philosophisin! That's whit we did fir kicks. No women. There had tae be somethin tae read, fir fuck's sake. Ah looked through the mess on the bedroom flair fir somethin – onythin. An then, underneath a pile ay shitty laundry ah fund a battered paperback ay Bertrand Russell an ah fell oan it wi a frenzy. Cannae stand the wee atheist gobshite – whit's wi aw that Celestial Teapot bollocks onyhow? – but philosophers cannae be choosers.

So ah settled doon oan the settee an as soon as ah started readin aw thae gorgeous words ah felt ma pulse settlin back intae somethin like a normal rhythm. The familiar ooze ay thoughts an ideas started birlin aboot ma heid. Reality be buggered. Pure fuckin magic, ken?

I'd hae been okay if it hadnae been for that fuckin heidbang Nietzsche comin roon. Trouble wi that bam is he's that fuckin sure ay himsel. Ye'd think a bastart whit spent the last twenty years ay his life in a fuckin loony bin widnae be so cocksure, eh? But no oor Freddyboy. 'Achtung! Achtung! I teach you ze Superman, zeig heil.' Aye well, Superman can skite up Lois Lane's arse an droon in keech for aw ah care. An as for the hammer speakin, I'd like tae stick it straight doon his radge throat.

An me a peace lover, an aw.

Ah shouldnae huv answered the door. Ah kent fine it wid be him. But ah'm a fool, ay have been, cannae see a fellow man in distress withoot takin his pain ontae masel. It's ma curse, ken?

'Christ, cunt,' he said, bargin past me, 'ah need a fix.'

'Aye, me an aw. Any mair ay this an ah'll be reduced tae readin Paulo fuckin Coelho.'

'Whit time does the cuntin library open?'

'No till half nine. Cutbacks.'

'Fuckin cooncil. Bunch ay cuntin philistines. Got any books?'

'Russell. A bit ay Sartre in the cludgie.'

Nietzsche smacked me one on the pus. 'Ye can fuck yer Sartre,' he said. 'Cunt. Ah saw him doon Princes Street

Gardens the ither day, jist starin at trees. Whit's that aw aboot?'

'Nothin wrang wi starin at trees, Freddyboy. Best days ay ma life were spent observin nature.'

'Ay, wid that be sixteen-year-auld nature?'

'Dinnae start malignin me, ye heidbang. Ye're like awbody else, ye've got it in fir puir Jean-Jacques.'

'Ach, shut up, ye Swiss cunt.' Nietzsche rifled through the pages ay the Russell, shakin his heid an tutsing like a Nun at an orgy. 'Heap ay crap,' he said an flung it against the far wa. 'Here,' he said, 'jist look at ma shakes. Sure ye're no holdin oot on me, Jane-Jacqueline?'

Ah kept shtoom. Aw ma life ah've had fowk tryin tae wind me up so's ah've learned tae ignore it. Nietzsche wis a big bugger, though, frightenin, ken, fuckin hairy, wi a beard that hadnae been trimmed in ten year, an mair hair up his nose than ah hiv on ma heid. Maist fowks wis scared enough tae shit a nappy if he gave them evils. Aye, an whinever his *Zarathustra* sprach yon auld bollocks they'd jist nod their heids an fuck aff sharpish. No me, though. Ah cannae stoap masel. It's anither ay ma curses. Ah get intae fights, get masel beat up, an then ah feel sorry fir the bastart afterwards, in case ah hurt his knuckles oan ma face.

'Ye havenae had that wee cunt Plato hangin roond here, have ye?' he said. He seemed tae take up mair space than there actually wis in the room. It wis like he wis everywhere at once. Ah shook ma heid. Plato wis persona non fuckin grata roon the estate since he started passing aff his ain stuff as Socrates's. Freddy wis bangin his heid against the wa. Ah didnae like the look ay it. He wis buildin himsel up fir a big ain, ah could tell.

'Ah saw him ootside,' he said, 'skulking aboot. "Awa back tae yer cave, ya cunt," ah shouted at him. Ken whit he said back?' Ah shook ma heid. '"Hoi Nietzsche, how do ah ken ye even exist?"'

'Ye didnae nut him?'

'Too fuckin right ah nutted the cunt. Doon like a sack ay tatties. Busted nose an aw. "Well ye fuckin ken noo," ah says tae him. Radge cunt. Fuck it man, ah need some real gear. Whit time is it noo?'

'No even half eight. Calm doon, for fuck's sake.'

But he wis aye impetuous, Nietzsche. He had aw thae fancy fuckin notions aboot bein hard an seizin the moment an a that shite. Basketcase if ye ask me. Me, ah wis mair happy tae tak a walk doon the river an contemplate the beauty ay nature. There's mair satisfaction in watchin a heron staunin on wan leg in the watter than in watchin the throng ay humanity hurl their way doon the Gorgie Road tae Tynecastle for an efternin's mindless violence. But ye couldnae make Freddyboy see that. He saw thae scum wi their Jam Tarts an Hibees scarves an said they jist proved his fuckin point – proles, waitin for their Superman tae come an lead them.

'Ach, fuck this fir a game ay teleology,' he said. He grabbed ma lapel an flung me ootma chair. 'Get yer arse thigither, Jacqueline. We're breakin intae that library.' He puffed oot his chest an gave his best Superman swagger. 'They'll no keep us frae oor books. We are PHILOSOPHERS!'

Ah said no, of course, but 'nein' isnae in Freddyboy's vocabulary. We were ootside Leith Library within ten minutes, me wi a brick in ma haund an him wi a sneer the size ay the Forth Road Bridge.

'Why dae ah hiv tae throw the brick?' ah said.

'Cos you're the noble savage, Janey.'

It fair gets ma goat when fowk misquote me like that. Ah nivver said we should aw be noble savages – ah said the exact fuckin opposite. Savages we can be, aye, but noble, nae way. One look at the queue doon the broo proves that.

'An you're the fuckin Superman,' ah said.

'Pit it this way, Judy. Either you hurl the brick through

the windae, or carry on haudin it an ah'll hurl you through the windae. It amounts tae the same.' Christ, he wis big. An nasty. Wi a tendency tae say whit he meant, ken.

Ah hurled the brick through the windae. Right away these fuckin alarms started screamin, aw ower the shop. Folks stopped tae stare. Cars an aw. Gridlock. An me the shy, retirin type.

'Come on, Jasmine. We are philosophers an we need tae read.'

He walked through the broken windae, no botherin tae clear away the shards stuck in the frame an they gashed intae him. Blood wis pulsin doon his face as he marched on, past the romances an crimes an poetry tae the philosophy section. Ah hurried after, tryin no tae think ay masel as some kind ay mere follower. Jean-Jacques leads, he disnae follow. But Freddy had the scent ay philosophy in his nostrils an he wis gallopin doon the libray like a dug chasin a rabbit.

'Ye wouldnae fuckin believe it!' he yelled. 'Cunts. Take a swatch at thae shelves, Jennifer.'

'Whit is it?' ah said.

'It's no whit it is, it's whit it isnae. No a single ain ay ma books on thae shelves. Cunts. Ignorant fuckin serfs.'

Ah looked. He wis right enough. An worse, there wis nane ay my books either.

'Bastarts,' ah said.

'Ah mean,' he said, an he hud his daunder up big time noo. 'Ah mean, Foucault. Lacan. Cuntin French cunts. Whit the fuck dae they ken aboot fuckin philosophy? Zizek? That's no a name, that's a fuckin sneeze. *Philosophy ay the real*? Show his face roon here, ah'll show the cunt fuckin real. He'll be feelin it till fuckin doomsday.'

Ah sighed. 'Ach Friedrich,' ah said, feeling suddenly auld an tired. 'Whit is life but a process ay change an decay? There's naethin permanent, ma son.'

Nietzsche booted the bookshelf, toppling it wi an almighty

clatter. Books fuckin aw place, years ay dust scatterin in the air.

'Ay, Jean-Jacques. Ye're fuckin right fir once. Aw they modern cunts. They forget the past. Or worse than that they fuckin rewrite it the way they want. They forget aw aboot us. The sacrifices we made. Fuckin leaps ay genius. If it wisnae for us they'd still be in mud fuckin huts.'

I thought that wis a bit much, but he had that look that said dinnae fuckin argue. In the distance ah could hear sirens. Freddy sooked in a lungful ay air.

He started kickin *The History ay Hibernian Fitba Club* aboot the floor an then whanged it through the broken windae. *Clematis fir yer Gairden* followed, an *Plumbin for Dummies*. The soond ay the sirens wis comin closer.

'We'll hae the last fuckin laugh, though,' he said. 'It'll be oor turn again wan day. Aw this life ay misery will start up again an Friedrich will be returned tae his place ay honour, the *Übermensch*.'

Noo, ah always thought this perpetual return jobby wis where Freddy lost the plot, but he wis fair stuck oan the notion. Life replayin itself ower an ower. Sounded like a fuckin nightmare tae me. Ah couldnae bear the thought ay ma life startin ower. Lovin an losin Mme de Warens again. Nae way. Aye, we were a right pair, me an Freddy. The outcast an the lunatic.

'Mind you,' he said, 'when ah defined that theory ay perpetual return, ah didnae realise it wis gonnae be in a cuntin Leith cooncil estate.'

'No classy, is it? Could it no hae been Corstorphine?'

'Ach naw, that's ower near the zoo. Stinks tae buggery. Aw that elephant shit. Ah mean, dis that no jist prove there's nae God? Whit's the point ay elephant shit?'

'Of course there's a point tae elephant shit. If ye didnae hae elephant shit the elephants wid explode. Can ye imagine how mingin that wid be, walkin doon the Royal Mile in yer finery an ye get a swatch ay rancid elephant trunk hurled ontae yer visage? Or impaled on a flyin fuckin tusk? Jist ma fuckin luck that wid be.'

The sirens were right ootside. The noise wis deafenin. Ah couldnae even hear Freddyboy's rantin fir it, so that wis a mercy at least. There wis polis cars aw ower the place. Must hae been a slack day in Embra.

'Come oot wi yer haunds up,' this voice birled through a megaphone.

'Awa an stick yer heids up yer jaxxie,' shouted Freddy.

'See yous fuckin philosophers,' the megaphone roared, 'ye're aw the fuckin same. Nothin but trouble since ye came here. Third time this week this libray's been ransacked. That tosser Aristotle's still doon the station. D'ye ken anyone whit speaks Greek?'

'Cretin!' shouted Freddy. 'We philosophers are here tae save mankind fae itsel.'

'Yer arse in parsley! Wha saves mankind fae yous tossers?'

Freddieboy started siftin through the debris on the flair, pickin up aw the philosophy that wisnae by some French bastart.

'We're better aff withoot yous,' the megaphone continued. 'Can yous no aw fuck off back tae where ye came fae an leave us honest fowks alane? We dinnae want yer philosophy. We dinnae want tae be saved.'

'Fuckin ingrates!' ah shouted. Freddy wis busy stashing books under his oxters, doon his shirt, in his Ys, ony place he could fit them.

'Come oan, Jessica,' he said. 'Help.'

'Whit are ye daein?'

'We need some readin for later. We'll need a cuntin fix.'

'Christ, Freddy, there's a difference between scratchin yer arse an rippin it tae shreds. We dinnae need that much.'

'Come oan,' he said. 'Make a break fir it.' He waddled tae

the windae like the Michelin Man hid pished itsel.

'Wha do ye think we are?' ah said. 'Butch an fuckin Sundance?'

'Well, ye're no Butch, onyway. Come oan Sundance…'

'Ach, come oan then, Butch.'

We pushed through the windae ontae Leith High Street, trailin philosophy in oor wake. We made it past Costa Coffee an Waterstones an HMV an burst ontae The Parade. Sprintin like, intae the gloamin. Ah hud the wind in ma sails noo. No bad for a twa-hundert year deid philosopher, eh? This is the life, ah thought. Aye, choose freedom. Choose happiness. Choose tae stick twa fingers up at the snotty-nosed bitch in the Lexus giein us the horn. Choose tae smile. Choose life.

Aye, right.

Choose the memory ay Mme de Warens over any dusty fuckin treatise on yer social contract. Choose romance. Choose tae speak the words ay romance. Ah luv ye, hen.

Choose tae run intae the sunset. Choose Applegarth Street instead ay Potson Road. Choose the street hoachin wi fuckin polis.

Choose tae pit yir haunds up. Haunds oot. Handcuffs oan. Choose tae look at Freddyboy, sat oan the pavement, greetin intae his beard. Man is born free, some twat once said. Oh, it wis me. Aye, an he is everywhere in chains. Up fuckin Leith way he is, onyhow. D'ye ken whit ah'd choose, if ah only could? If ah could hae ma life ower again, ah'd choose that it wis different.

That's aw.

Joss'n'Jules Forever

That morning, final morning, first Wednesday of August 1985, Joss'n'Jules prepared for their outing. Joss selected his most garish outfit, outrageous in purple and red. He ate a Gordon and Durward's sugar mouse in two bites and helped it down with black coffee. Jules brushed his teeth, grimacing at the minstrel mouth facing him in the mirror. He counted to fifty, then to one hundred, trying to divorce his mind from his body, to gain relief, if only for a few moments. He wiped down his face, clicked his back into position and limped to the living room.

'Have you been sick?' said Joss.

'Yes.'

'It'll be that pizza last night. Looked undercooked to me.'

Jules nodded. 'Probably,' he said. 'Never used to happen. In the old days.'

'They didn't have pizza in the old days.'

'They must have done. In Italy.'

'We've never been to Italy.'

'No.'

In days past such conversation, trivial, convivial, could have been extemporised until mid-morning and beyond. It would have been a diversion, their wordplay jazzing down ever more implausible byways into the purely fantastic. Today, it expired into silence. Joss poured milk down the sink and piled the contents of the fridge into a bag and placed it in the bin outside. Jules took red roses from their vase and placed them on the composting bay in the garden. They looked round their flat, small and tidy, light, peaceful. Photographs on the walls, so many, so neat, Joss'n'Jules through a lifetime of activity and entertainment. The common thread was happiness. Nothing is ever so serious, Joss once said, that a frown should eclipse a smile.

'Ready?' he said now. His smile was at its most sardonic, his eyes their most mischievous. His hat was tilted at the jauntiest of angles. They kissed and held hands until the silence became too loud. They looked at the grandfather clock stilled in the hallway.

'Time,' said Jules.

'Time,' said Joss.

Time pulsed around them, time in its cruelty. Joss Stein and Jules Sartorius thought synchronous thoughts, life distilled into its essence, the transit of love. Remember? First meeting, first kiss, first proclamation? Two lifetimes fused in history, inconsequential to all but them. *For* them, everything. It is seldom the grandest memories which surface in such moments and Joss recalled an afternoon by the river Earn in the early nineteen-sixties, lying on the bank beside Jules and staring at the sky. A cloud drifted by, a single cloud in an otherwise pristine expanse, and the sun was momentarily occluded and he felt a chill on his bare arm. It lasted no more than twenty seconds but he could recall it now as though it had only just happened.

Jules looked at the living room and remembered it as they first saw it, empty, dirty, an experience waiting to be inhabited, and the two of them at the start of their great adventure.

'Thirty years,' he said as the door creaked behind them and they stood in the dark passageway.

'You'd think we'd have found time to oil that hinge,' said Joss. They descended the stairs and entered the bustle of Crieff High Street. Half a dozen people spoke to them and they replied with courtesy and no little wit. Bob Kelty was visible through the window of Cloudland. He waved.

'I think Bob's cleaned the windows,' said Jules.

'Or wiped off the grease, anyway.'

As ten o'clock struck Joss tortured their Ford Fiesta into starting and they journeyed twenty miles towards Perth. Only twice did approaching cars feel the need to flash their lights as Joss, unconcerned which side of the white line he occupied, veered towards them. Joss gave them a cheery wave and carried on regardless. The car park at Kinnoull Hill was quiet enough for him to effect a final manoeuvre in relative safety and he rolled the Fiesta to a halt close to a parking bay. He switched off the engine and stared ahead.

'Here we are,' he said.

'Here we go.'

It was silent except for bird song and wind whisper. The sky was clear, the air sharp. It would be hot later but for now there was a chill. They left the car unlocked. Jules's stomach no longer ached, no longer felt full of gravel and cement and desperation. It happened like that some days, hours of blessed nothingness before the pain returned, redoubled, burnishing itself on his psyche. The physical relief of such times served only to reinforce the mental pain, like the phantom ache of a severed limb.

'It's a beautiful day,' he said.

'All our days are beautiful,' said Joss. 'In their way.'

'In our way.'

'In our way.'

They walked ahead, muffled in overcoats and scarves. Jules coughed, Joss limped. Two crows flew above them. A magpie strolled on the grass alongside. A sharp wind pulsed from the east.

'I'm cold,' said Jules.

'You should have worn more clothing.'

'More clothing wouldn't have helped.'

'It wouldn't have hindered.'

They climbed, slowly, stopping regularly to feign interest in whatever lay before them, rosebay willowherb rising high and pink, thistles alongside, whins of turquoise blue, sharp-tined and malevolent, broom scabbed with black seed pods, hogweed white as bones in the high sun. Grass and more grass and more grass. Soon it would all turn, autumn landing, the end approaching. They walked on.

'We should have gone to Italy,' said Joss. 'Once.'

'Very wet this year, I hear.'

'We're Scottish. Rain doesn't frighten us.'

The hill was deserted except for them. It made the slowness of their passage less obvious. Jules cramped halfway up, doubling over for a few painful seconds, gasping for breath, trying not to be sick. He pulled himself straight and smiled and looked at the world as though a stranger and they walked on.

At the top of Kinnoull Hill, highest point for miles, the wind gusted and circled. The light was pale. Around them, the Strathearn valley lay revealed, fields resolving into green and gold and yellow, hedges and dykes, stands of oak and beech and birch, the river's eccentric meander, lazy like the unfurling of eternity. Before them the hill plunged sheer and deep, granite dropping two hundred feet into the void. Neither looked at the other. There was no need, symbiosis, unbreakable.

'You can see for miles,' said Joss.

'You can see forever.'

'Forever's not as far as you think.'

'I never thought to hear you say something like that, Mr Tomorrow.' Jules's voice was light and teasing.

'There's always tomorrow,' said Joss, 'but at some stage it becomes today and today turns into yesterday and there's nothing you can do to stop it.'

'Junctions.'

'I think this is a junction.'

'No, it's a hill.'

'Ho ho ho. We must remember that one.'

'I remember the first time we came here. Must be thirty years ago. Thirty-five?'

'It was 1949, Jules.'

'It was?'

'Twenty-first of June, 1949.'

'You remember that?'

'Of course.'

'I didn't realise.'

'You told me you loved me.'

'You told me you loved me.'

'I always will.'

'I always have.'

'I love you.'

'I love you.'

'Together.'

'Forever.'

'Love you today.'

'Love you tomorrow.' Jules looked around. There were tractors and combine harvesters in the fields, men working, bringing the season to an end. A jackdaw sat in a beech tree. Blaeberry bushes all around were ripe with fruit. A rabbit ran. Lives were lived.

'It's just too hard,' he said. 'I'm sorry, I can't do it any longer.'

Once there was a young man called Jules Sartorius. He was strikingly clever. Beautiful. Poised. He wrote music and sang songs that could make people cry with happiness. He fell in love with his opposite, his correlative, Joss Stein, and together they lived in laughter and dreams. Whatever happened to Jules Sartorius, fine young man? His head thrummed with the pulsing of his blood. His limbs were heavy but his body felt light. He saw but he could no longer absorb the images. They made no sense. They were no longer part of him.

He looked at Joss and smiled. He kissed him once, softly, on the lips. He stepped towards the edge with a nimbleness he hadn't known for thirty years and looked down at the trees stretching into the distance, world at rest. Beyond, a ribbon of roadway transporting people through their lives. Further on the Tay flowing unstoppably. He stepped forward, into air. He fell, straight downwards, and it was quick and graceful, seventy yards, and he landed on his feet as though he expected to walk away to inspect the nearby shrubbery.

Joss looked down for a moment, then away. He bit his lip. He looked at the sky one last time. Clouds and blue. Chill on his arm. He remembered. Savoured the moment. He sat heavily on the edge of the hill and closed his eyes.

'Joss'n'Jules forever,' he said.

He rolled forward and then he, too, was gone.

And, far below, a blackbird began to sing in a nearby birch tree. It stopped. It took fright and flew off and circled a scene that had blown up in an instant.

Peewit

They walked slowly, cresting the hill at the Hosh and walking alongside the Shaggie Burn until they reached a hollow. Above was a light wood. The grass was wild, flattened into hummocks by the wind. The old man stopped.

'Hear that? Thon loud shriek? That's a peewit.' He grabbed her arm, pointing. 'Doon there, see?'

The bird was sitting on its nest, virtually hidden in rush grass. Only the brisk twisting of its neck and a glint from its eye gave it away. They crouched and watched.

'You have some eyes,' said Ash. 'I'd never of seen that in a million years.'

'You're no meant to. Keep themsels to themsels. They can be richt show-offs, mind. You'll see soon enough. The male winnae be far away.' The old man put his hand to his eyes and surveyed the skies. 'There.'

They watched as a bird, black and white and green, swooped across the sky like a World War Two fighter ace, whooping all the time, a two-tone *peewit – peewit*. As it banked away from them it seemed to turn completely black and then, when it veered back towards them its chest and upper wings gleamed white in the sky. Its wingbeats were fast and exaggerated, like something pretending to be a bird. Thrilling.

'Mrs Peewit must get real bored, jes sittin around on those eggs all day, while he's off havin fun.'

'Aye, she'll be there for up to a month.'

'Shit. No way I'd do that.'

'I hate to tell you, but you'll be at it nine month when it's your time.'

'Not me. Ain't havin' no kids, noway.'

'You say that noo. But you'll get to an age when you want them, so they can do better than you. Get right what you got wrong.'

'Hey, didn't you know? I'm perfect already.'

He smiled. 'Aye, maybe. Thon peewit's a very particular bird, though. Want to see?'

Ash nodded and the old man stood up and beckoned to her to follow. He walked towards the peewit's nest, hallooing and waving his arms until the bird finally, reluctantly, flew off.

There were three smallish blotchy brown eggs in the unguarded nest. He turned each round by ninety degrees. 'Now, mind the position they're in,' he said. They walked back to the top of the hollow and leaned against a silver birch and watched.

The peewit circled a couple of times and returned to its nest. It flitted around as though unable to settle. After a few moments it sat motionless once more, silent in splendid observance.

For a second time they approached and the bird rose again and swooped towards the wood.

'Noo,' he said. 'What do you see?'

It took Ash a moment, but then her frown turned to a smile. 'It's turned the eggs back again.'

'Aye, it ay does. Cannae bear to sit on eggs if they're no in the richt position.'

Ash laughed. 'How did you learn things like that?'

'Just workin the land. D'you want these eggs for your breakfast?'

'No. I couldn't bear to think of that poor momma bird comin back to an empty nest.'

'You're ower soft,' said the old man, but he was relieved. He knew the show-off daddy bird would have been equally bereft.

Sequela

Mally Vogel stared at the blue-black sky unfolding above him, moving image of eternity. His mouth was dry and rank. He had a pain in his left shoulder and the rest of his body was sore. He tried to move but couldn't. Smell of earth in his nostrils. Dampness. Cold. A dark wall rose above him on either side, earth, grass, roots. *Am I in my grave?* he thought. *Is it over?* As he lay there the last of the night stars disappeared one by one, darkness resolving into day. There were birds. Clouds gathering, rain threatening. Mally Vogel stared upwards, tried to move, tried to think.

He knew if he didn't get out of here soon he would die. His difficulty was he had no idea where he was.

Or how he'd got there.

He was accustomed to a chasm of confusion in the mornings, that void where memory should be, the despair that accompanied the return of consciousness. But this was different. Normally, he would wake in the house, the drunkard's homing instinct ensuring safe passage. Even when he didn't make it home he would wake up in MacRosty Park, or James Square, or a doorway. Not in a hole in the ground.

What happened yesterday? What had he done? He stared upwards and tried to focus his mind. An image came to him. Sitting in his Jaguar. Nobody on the streets. There was rain. Another disappointment bore down on him. He was driving on the Muthill straights, night as dark as death. The speedometer hit the ton. As he climbed towards the bends at the Drummond Castle estate he kept the Jag pointed straight ahead. This was how he'd imagined it dozens of times, the one hundred miles per hour impact freeing him from all future responsibility.

It didn't happen. He steered round the bend, coward to the last. So what happened next? Had he crashed? Had incompetence achieved what he wasn't brave enough to do by himself? He listened and couldn't hear traffic and didn't think he was near a road. He tried to lift his hand but couldn't feel it. There was a pain in his face as though his skin was burning. He wanted to touch it, soothe it. He lay motionless instead.

Your name is Mally Vogel. You're a loser. If you really are dying no-one will care. Your wife will cheer and your kids will shrug their shoulders. Your friends won't be surprised. He had it coming, they'll say. Only a matter of time.

Something bad happened. He knew it but couldn't locate it. It was always this way. He'd wake with a gnawing guilt in his stomach and no way of identifying what had caused it, shame exacerbated by ignorance. *Narrow down the possibilities, Mally. It'll involve Angela. It always does.* He heard something rustling in the undergrowth that was somehow above him.

'Go away,' he tried to say, but he could barely hear himself. 'Please.'

A long face appeared above him, red and whiskery, dark eyes staring impassively at the improbable sight beneath. It was beautiful, so confident and sleek. The fox studied him in silence for some moments before it turned and disappeared and Mally felt a desolation worse than anything he had ever experienced. It was darker than any of the darkest moments of this darkest year that had started on Hogmanay in intensive care in Perth Royal Infirmary having his jaw reassembled. It was to end, it seemed, here, now, in June, in dissolution, in ruin.

'Mally Vogel's an intelligent boy but he leads himself astray.' 'Mally has an addictive personality which will surely get him into trouble.' 'Mally Vogel's teeth are black, he looks like shite and smells like cack.' Mally Vogel, butt of everyone's jokes, the boy least likely, the man least able.

A loser dying in a ditch.

'You've gone too far this time, Mally.'

Don't I always?

There was an argument with Angela. He'd told her he was going to commit suicide. 'Run the Jag into a wall. There'll be nothing left of me. That's best.'

Attention-seeking bastard. Every time he did it he told himself it would be the last. It never was.

'I'm calling the police.'

Angela and the kids were staying with Angela's sister in Commissioner Street. Isobel. Sanctimonious bitch. It was her poisoning Angela's mind, turning her against him. It was her fault. Whenever Angela looked at him now there was hatred in her eyes. And pity. Alice and Graeme, eight and seven, no longer wanted to see their daddy. They were scared of him. He said things that were cruel or nasty or didn't make sense. He staggered about the house. He smelled. He wasn't funny like he used to be, didn't play with them, didn't make up bedtime stories. And the more distant his family grew the more Mally took refuge in whisky and the cycle spiralled downwards and down. This was hell.

'Call them. I'll resist arrest. They can beat me up. You'd like that, wouldn't you?'

'You've wrecked my sister's house, you bastard.'

Rain started to fall and he opened his mouth and let the drops refresh his parched tongue and throat. A belt of pain around his temples was tightening. There was a pigeon sitting in a nearby tree, cooing constantly. *Crazy... we're all going crazy... we're all going...* Mally tried to ignore it but the harder he tried the more insistent it grew. It was as though the noise was in his head, as though the pigeon was inside him, haunting him, taunting. It would be there always. The rain grew heavier. It was sharp and hard, not like June rain at all. Mally's already cold body grew colder. He started to cry.

He hadn't resisted arrest, had he? Otherwise, how could he have gone out in the car afterwards? Two policemen called, one old, the other younger. The memory began to unfold, moment by moment. Seated on his settee, trying to focus on them, trying to understand what they were saying. Following them into the police car, into the station, into the interview room. 'Mally Vogel, I am formally charging you with criminal damage...'

Mally moaned. His clothes were soaked. Rain was running down his face in rivulets, the tickling sensation driving him mad. There was a pain in his chest like his heart was being repeatedly punched. Was it a heart attack? Was this how it would end? *Please, please.*

Afterwards, they drove him home. *That was kind.* 'You need to sort yourself out, sir. There's a Perth branch of Alcoholics Anonymous. I would recommend...'

He drank another half bottle of whisky after they left. Or was it a whole bottle? Jesus Christ, no wonder he was in this state. Even for Mally that was a heavy session. It had been about three in the morning when he took the Jag out. Later maybe.

He went over it again. 'I am formally charging you with criminal damage.' What criminal damage? 'You've wrecked my sister's house, you bastard.' Mally closed his eyes, forced himself to think. He was round the back of her sister's house. Up a ladder. In the bathroom window. He got stuck, his upper body through the window but without the leverage to pull his legs up. There was a dog barking, the sound of footsteps approaching and then receding. He gripped the edge of the sink and pulled himself through. The weight of his whole body rested on the sink and it gave way and Mally tumbled headfirst into the bathroom and landed on top of it. There was a hissing sound and he could feel his clothes getting wet and he turned round to see what was causing it. The sink had been pulled from the wall and the pipe was ruptured. Water was pulsing out of it in a torrent. He put his hand against it and water sprayed all over his face. He swore and pulled his hand away.

'Fuck.'

He ran downstairs and opened the front door and looked out. The street was empty and he bolted. Didn't even close the door. Now, working through the memory of it, he couldn't fathom what he was doing there anyway. Why was he breaking into his sister-in-law's house? That made no sense.

Nothing about you makes sense, Vogel. You're a moron. You've flooded her house, you cretin. You deserve this. Rain was sheeting down and he could feel the water rising around him. *You're going to drown. Just deserts.* He stared at the greyness above him and closed his eyes but still saw light bearing down on him like a curse. He felt both inside and outside the world, as though, simultaneously, he was hurtling towards the end and the end was speeding towards him.

'What on earth?'

Mally could feel something splashing about at his feet. He looked down to see a spaniel nosing around at his boots. He groaned.

'What are you doing in there?' A terrified face stared down at him, an old woman in a sodden headscarf. She stared at him with incomprehension. He stared back. 'Wait there, I'll get help. Kit, come on, boy.'

Mally shook his head. *Please no,* he thought. *Please don't get help. Leave me here.* He still had no notion of where he was but he was reconciled to it. He was calm. The pain in his head had eased and the pain in his chest was growing but otherwise he was completely numb.

It was the most relaxed Mally Vogel had felt in months.

The Rational Matters of Rational Men

Now my forebears were superstitious folks. That's juist the wey they were. This is back in the last century, of course, in the auld Queen's time, and they saw nothin unusual in believin in fairies and wild mountain men or witches and goblins or the prattlins of weird-men and spae-wives. The natural and the supernatural, they were all the same, back then. But they didnae hae the books, you see, nor the learnin that goes wi the books, and so it's understandable. They're no to be laughed at. It doesnae do for a rational man to laugh at the irrational acts of others.

I'm sayin all this by wey of preface to the story I'm aboot to relate to you, for those of an irrational nature micht tak fae it fanciful notions, and that's no my intention at all. I'm simply explainin what happened, as weel as I'm able, and if there's onythin that cannae be understood then that is the fault of my poor comprehension only, and no the result of some supernaturalistic foolery.

It was juist afore the fourteen-eighteen war I would say. Things were different then, quieter, slower. I had nae idea that a war would be startin forthwith, nor why, and still I dinnae ken the cause of all that, if truth be kent. Aye, and there was another war in 1939, and they say the third ane is on its wey, what wi the killin of thon Kennedy fellow the other day, but the causes of sic things are mysteries to me. I sit in my wee howff in the Cuillins and think of the strangeness of it all, and if we are to be only meenits fae destruction would it really be so bad? No noo that my world has shrunk to this, no, but back then the mountain was mine, I suppose you could say. No literally, mind, the mountain is the mountain, beholden to nae man, but this was afore the tourists and the climbers and those foolish holidayin folks started to tear it up.

Well onywey, I was makin my way through the Lhearre Pass, headin for the village at the end of the Corrie Vrech where I had some business wi the factor. It was a twa day hike, mind, even in grand weather, which it was shapin up no to be, but I had it in mind to overnight at the bothy near the Witch's Cauldron. It was a fine bothy, that ain, very popular wi the deer-stalkers afore the war for it was dry as tinder, and wi a rare supply of bogwood for lightin the fire. Aye, it was a grey mornin, though, the cloud all aroond and no a view to be seen. You walk fae memory on days such as those, and I was perhaps an hoor in when I saw twa fellows emergin fae the mirk and they were almost upon me afore I kent it.

'Hello,' said ane.

'Hello,' said I. As they came into view it looked to me like Sandy Murray but it couldnae be him for he was in Pitlochry for the start of the trout fishin, as weel I kent.

'Is it Jock Menzies?' said he and I said it was and he said he was Archie Murray, Sandy Murray's brother, and so it was, for was he no the very likeness? His companion, he telt me, was his cousin fae Arrachar, Willie Robertson.

'You've a fair load on you,' said I, for they were baith carryin their kit on their backs and they looked like they must be headin for Inverness, so laden were they. Aye, they said, they were in the bothy at the Witch's Cauldron for the shootin, but they needed supplies so they were goin doon to the village to fetch them.

'We're comin back the night,' said Sandy Murray's brother and I gave him a quizzical look. 'We didnae want to leave oor things in the bothy, unprotected,' said he.

Well, you could hae left the jewels of Scotland in thon

bothy back in thae days, and it would be waitin aa the while for the next King of Scots to collect them, but I didnae like to say, for they looked fair trauchled already.

'Rain,' said I. 'Comin ower the valley. You'd best be quick.'

'Aye,' said Sandy Murray's brother, 'we'll awa.'

'I'm off to the bothy mysel,' said I, 'I'll get you a fire goin. Gie my regards to Aisling Campbell in the village store. Tell her I'll be back in fower days at most.'

'For sure,' said Sandy Murray's brother. 'And that sounds like a message of romance, if I'm no mistaken.'

'Indeed it is not.' And I stalked away at the hurry, irritated by the impertinence of the man. The dullness of the day still hung low and it was cauld enough to rattle the banes. February does that to the weather: it's a short month but vicious, like a fishwife in a hurry. And so I sang some sangs on my journey, for did my mither no say that sweet music was the finest wey to part the cloods? Indeed so, she said, and it cleaved a righteous path into the skies towards the auld man himsel. Oh-ho, says you, and you think you've caught me oot, d'you no, thinkin you've trapped Jock Menzies in a contradiction? Believin in superstitions noo are we, Jock Menzies, after all you've juist been tellin us? No me, but it doesnae do to defy the mither, even wi her thirty year deid. And so still I sing sangs to the skies juist like she instructed, juist as I carry a lump of black coal on Hogmanay, juist as I check the cauld ashes of the Christmas fire on Boxin day morn for signs of what micht be. There's nae harm in harmless traditions, that's what I say.

Mention of my mither reminds me of my faither, for they were gey close. Noo my father was a fairmhand and skilled wi the horses and that made him popular wi all the fairmers aroond for he could manage the ploo better than maist, and so he moved fae fairm to fairm, ay in demand. He could tell some stories, my faither, no like me, and I mind one tale he telt aboot the Black Fairmer, as he was called, Campbell I believe his name was, but no relation of Aisling Campbell in the shoppie in the village, and if I close my eyes can I no see that lassie's bonnie face smilin at me once again? But dinnae tempt me doon such darkened alleys; what's past is done. So noo, we were talkin of Campbell the farmer: this would be, oh, a hundred year syne, maybe mair. Early in the reign of Victoria, I would fancy. Noo this Black Fairmer, he was in cahoots wi the deil, that's what folks said. He was a dangerous fellow and no to be broached, particularly on a dark nicht, or on a lonely road or in the time of the full moon. Why do you think folks thocht that about this man, my faither asked me. I met him mony a time, said he, and he ay seemed upright and decent and honest and true, but the stories they telt aboot him, aye they would mak your bluid freeze. I've nae idea, faither, I said to him. Tell me the truth of it.

And so my faither telt me: 'Jealousy, lad, what a curse the jealousy is.' See, Mr Campbell was a grand fairmer, he ran a fine fairm, and he ay had the best barley and the finest corn and the goldenest wheat and aabody looked at him in jealousy and said there must be some accountin for his growin thae crops so fine. And it was easier for those simple folks to think it was the deil at work than to wonder at how auld Campbell could coax a better crop than they fae the grund. And that was the truth of it. And no that long ago, either, scarce ninety year. I'm no even sure how different it would be the day and sad that is to say.

But a wee digression for you there, and me, I'm still walkin the mountain in this tale I'm tryin to relate to you. The weather was closin aroond me, ay denser, a fog as could smother your lungs and a dampness that clung to you like cleavers. I've stravaiged these mountains nye fifty year but I'm no too proud to admit that at times sic as those a man could get fearful lost. I kent the generality of my bearins, but as to the precise exactitude of it, I couldnae speak wi total confidence. Well noo, to be honest, I was completely flummoxed.

Walk on, man, thocht I. The fog wasnae so bad you could fall off a cliff wi-oot kennin it, so I was safe enough in my wee bit confusion. I had a sense of the direction I needed to be takin and followed my instinct, singin whiles loud enough for my throat to turn hoarse afore midday. And, sure enough, in the late efternoon the cloods began to clear. I'll no say it was my singin did it, other than in gentle jest, but as the sky started to keek through thon blanket of cover I sang louder than I ever had afore, and the soond of it was ringin through the valley and it left me in the grandest of humours.

Forbye, I could gather my bearins, and I was dumfoondit to discover I was much higher up the mountainside than I had realised. Heavens, I must hae climbed near twa hundert feet and to this day I dinnae ken how I managed it, and me scarcely oot of breath. But that was it and there I was, fair close to the summit itself. Why, wi juist a wee detour, I thoht to mysel, I could be there in an hoor and wi the weather clearin wi every passin minute, by the time I got there I'd hae mysel a grand view of the hale valley. My journeyin could surely contain itself a wee couple of hoors?

So I climbed to the very tap of the mountain and it was a strain on the knees and a test of the lungs but the air that had been thick and damp was noo fresh and crisp. I turned all arond to view Cairngorm in her finery. Let nae man destroy this, I thocht, let it ay be the wilderness that civilisation nor society nor rules nor regulations may shackle and tame. I became momentarily teary, I'll no deny.

But my peace soon evaporated. As I looked back doon the valley I had so recently stravaiged – and noo we come to the very point of the tale I'm relatin to you – I saw what can only be described as the queerest thing. It fair struck me dumb. Far doon the valley, whaur the land was level and threaded through by three or fower streams, there was a body laid oot on the grund. It was clear as day, for it was in ain of the deposits of auld snaw that collect in the various hollows and dips in the land and the blackness of it against the white of the snaw stood oot for all to see. Goodness, it must hae been twelve feet tall, maybe mair. What on earth, thocht I, and commenced to starin at it, tryin to fathom what it micht be. It was movin, of that I was certain. It seemed to be advancin slowly through the snaw in the general direction of the mountainside – that is to say, towards me. I felt my body chill wi a momentary fear that, in truth, micht hae lasted longer than moments. Oh, it was the fear of death itself, I freely admit. There are, of course, legends aplenty aboot the Big Grey Man of the mountains, but it's all superstition and claptrap and I was a rational man no given to foolishness such as that. But there it was, a body in the distance, a giant body forbye, and it was advancin towards me wi its airms ootstretched as though beckonin to me, as though in grand need of my attention or my assistance.

Now if I were a storyteller like my faither I could stretch this tale for anither half hoor and hae you on the edge of your wits, but that's no my wey, so I shall foreclose it this very instant. That was no giant, no Big Grey Man of the mountains. What it was, I noo ken, as a man of science and reason, was a brocken spectre. Aye, it's common enough, by all accoonts, and it's caused by the sun's rays ahint me hittin my back and projectin the grey shadow of my ain body far, far doon the mountainside, so that it seemed to be a separate presence. And so it was mysel I was seein, and how often are a man's ghosts nothin but the shadows of his own fashionin? A brocken spectre, my ain reflection lookin up at me and seemin, for all the world, like a wild man advancin to meet me.

I can understand it, aye. And it's in sic weys that common superstitions and myths are formed, so that innocent folks are fooled and cajoled by them into believin in nonsenses. But ae thing remains a mystery to me to this very day. If it was my ain shadow reflected, which I most certainly believe it was, then in what order of things was its airms ootstretched and wavin at me in so furious a fashion, when throughoot the hale episode I ken that my ain were straight doon by my side? It's a funny sort of reflection that moves mair than the shape that maks it, would you no say? However, I had nae time that day to ponder the mysteries of aa that. No, as I looked ower the valley I could see, far distant, the weather was closin in again, for does the rain no sweep by in bands, ane efter the other, up in these parts? Walk on, Jock Menzies, said I, walk on.

I never wore a coat, of course, nae need: you were either wet or you werenae. Well, I was wet that day, soaked to the banes and cauld to the marrow. Never was there a grander sicht than thon bothy, squat in the lee of the Cauldron. I made my wey inside to start up a fire, for which purpose there should hae been a supply of bogwood in the loft, for is it no a common courtesy to leave the bothy so supplied when you depart? Indeed it is, for wha's to say what a state the next fellow to arrive may be in, and your wee bittie patience and consideration may well be the very thing to save his life. But no a sliver of it could I find, and nae prospect of startin a fire wi-oot it.

Now, the wonderful thing aboot bogwood, and naebody minds this nooadays except auld anes like me, is that you can use it soppin wet. You start by breakin it into tiny fragments and that reveals the resin inside that's all that remains of oor prehistoric forests. That taks a flame very readily, as you micht imagine, and you place mair bits of wid on that and so and so, gradually breakin the wid into bigger chunks and feedin them to the flames and in that way you hae a roarin fire in nae time.

Aye, but I first had to collect the bogwood, and mind it

was foul ootside. I had my claes aff already for they were prodigiously wet and it was easier, so I reasoned, to juist go oot as I was to collect the wid. So off I went wi my boots on my feet and naethin else, oot into the rain and doon the hill half a mile to the bogs. I tell you it was cauld fit to scrape the skin aff your behookie but, even so, even though the mountains were as free of folk as Union Street on a Flag Day, I was peerin aboot, left and right, to mak sure naeone could see me wanderin aboot in the buff. And, naturally, I saw no a soul exceptin a roe deer in the distance that, so long as I let it be, wouldae hae borne me any mind clothed or naked.

Whiles, I gathered enough bogwood and made my wey back up the hill to the bothy, and the thocht of a roarin fire made my heart gledsome. I sat on my hunkers and fed the bogweed onto the fire and lit it and aye, it was ablaze in nae time, and I made mysel a fine supper wi a bittie oatmeal. I could hae done wi a wee salmon to go alangside but the rain had pit paid to that notion, so I settled by the fire wi a cuppie tea and a pipe and my book and my ain thochts.

Night comes doon fast in the mountains, especially in February. It's the grandest time, a noble time, when nature taks ower and man must do its biddin. There's mony a fool sees ghosts and bawkies in the dusk but it's only the shiftin of the shade they're seein, that and their ain foolish fears. There was only ae window in the bothy, at the back, so I stood in the doorway for a half hoor, watchin the licht fade to grey and then to black and the fullness of the Lhearre Pass settled itself ower the bothy until dawn. There was nae wey that Sandy Murray's brother and Sandy Murray's cousin would find their wey back there this nicht. I finished my pipe and had a jimmy riddle against a rowan tree, then went back inside, pullin the ooter door ahint me and snappin the inside bar into place. I shut the inner door, too, and settled mysel for the night, wi a candle and my book by the fireside.

I was in nae hurry to go to sleep because there was nae bed left in the bothy. There used to be a grand auld wooden frame and a fine mattress, but some damned fool must hae burned them ae cauld nicht. There was some heather in the corner that the shooters must hae used the nicht afore, but that would mean a stiff neck for me in the mornin, for all that I was still a young man then. I settled instead wi Thomas Reid and began to read his *Essays On The Intellectual Powers*. It would be fower years, possibly, I'd been readin it at that time, and it was beginnin to mak a glimmer of sense. I had fond notions, perhaps in a further ten year of research, of obtainin fae it a grand understandin of the rational matters of rational men. Fifty year on and I still havenae finished it, but I'm comin to understand it, if only a little. Aye, back then, though, I considered mysel to be of good judgement in everyday coonsel and it seemed to me quite richt that we hae power ower our ain actions, what wise folk would call the determination of oor will. And I kent, too, though I joined in only rarely, that there was life and wit in my fellow folks, such as those doon the valley in the village. Aye, indeed, doon there, in her faither's hoose, there she'd be, flighty Aisling Campbell, and maybe it was juist the vanity but I was sure that she'd be sittin and starin into her ain wee fire and her thochts would like enough be upon me, Jock Menzies. For the lassie was besotted and nae mistake.

Sic were the thochts goin through my mind, a combination of the educational and the speculative, for nae man is perfect. As I sat by the fire I heard the front door slam shut. Queer, thocht I, for the nicht is as quiet as the grave up in the mountain and my hearin was keen but I hadnae heard a soul comin towards the bothy. I waited for the inner door to open but when it didnae I got up and opened it mysel. The ooter door was shut fast and I pulled at it, but it was barred on the ootside. Noo, how could that hae happened, I thocht to mysel. I wasnae frightened, as such, but it was a curious notion, a door that locked itsel. I wondered whether some gowk was playin cantrips, but there was naebody here but me. I pushed and pushed at it, thinkin maybe it was juist stiff in the frame, but it was locked shut, of that there was nae doobt.

And so, what could I dae? The windae in the back was only wee, but it opened ootweys and so I pulled mysel through and into the cauld of the nicht. There was a moon that hadnae been oot when last I looked, and wi that I could see enough to find my wey roond to the front and open the door. The bar had been locked shut, that was for sure. I looked aroond, walked doon to the river and the bog, up to the crags and roond the back of the bothy towards the clump of firs ahint and no a soul was there, no a livin thing was stirred that nicht wi the exception of me. It was maist peculiar.

'Damnation,' said I aloud and I apologised too, for profanity has nae place, no even in an empty wilderness. What would Aisling Campbell hae thocht of that sort of language? Back I went and unbolted the door and shut the windae. I had a good huddle at the fire while the warmth re-entered my banes, and still I couldnae fathom what had caused this commotion. Forbye, I decided to get some sleep. I sputtered oot the candle and settled onto the heather, which was better than I expected, there bein enough for twa men and so as soft to my body as my ain auld bed.

I kent, though, that afore I would get ony sleep I would hae to run the gauntlet of my thochts. Aye indeed, let me no be coy aboot it, for it is the women to whom I am referrin. Here was I, a man of thirty-seven and of sober disposition and long since settled. A rational man, no gien to fancies nor idle ways. I earned my passage through life wi the effort of my back and the skill of my haunds and the sharpness of my brain. Temptation had ignored me and I it, for that was a weakness I preferred no to confront. Aye but the temptation's easier to avoid when it's absent, and there's the truth. For when it's winkin its een at you fae across the coonter of Campbell's Stores and it's flatterin you wi fancy language, when the thocht of it is there at night, in the bed by your side and it's insinuatin itself like a worm in your ear, well the Deil himself micht as well be your opponent. Aye, the women, and nae mistake.

Forbye, though, I was driftin towards sleep and sloughin off the cares of the world when I heard the strangest soond. I can hear it still, a long, drawn oot voice, high-pitched, and it was whisperin my name, *Jock Menzies, Jock Menzies*. I lay still as a fox, liftin my heid to stop the heather rustlin by my ears. *Jock Menzies, Jock, Jock,* came the cry again, fae somewhere ootside, and I thocht I would die of fear. It was an unco sound and for certain the darkest moment of my life, for I had nae explanation for what was happenin, nor ony knowledge of what I should do next, and a rational man should ay hae an explanation and an action.

I've never been what you call a timid man, never afraid to confront a danger, but up until that moment I had ay kent what the danger was. Noo, the danger was a mystery, and I was that scared I was buryin myself in the heather to escape it. I wondered what Aisling Campbell would hae thocht to see me like thon. I pictured her watchin me. A brave man, she'd thocht me once. Noo look at me. She'd be sayin there's thon idiot Menzies gibberin into the heather, the auld fool who turned me doon last spring. For aye, that's what I did, and I cannae tell you why. It's like I lost control of my ain senses. The word 'no' fell oot of my gab afore I had a chance to think. I was feart, you see, and to this day I cannae tell you what it was aboot Aisling Campbell, the bonniest lass wha ever lived, that could hae frightened me.

As much to tak my mind off Aisling Campbell as to solve my problem, I thocht what Thomas Reid micht hae made of this. I lay in silence and considered a favourite passage of mine, ain I read maist weeks so it came to me fine enough, even in my fear. The only objects involved in thocht, he said, are in the world, no in the mind.

Aye, and then it came to me in a flash of inspiration, a moment of reason, no less. I pulled on my boots in the light of the fire and opened the inner and the ooter doors of the bothy to the nicht. 'Hello?' I shouted.

'Jock Menzies,' came the reply. It was comin fae doon the hill, towards the bog and it sounded like a whisper, made high and eerie by the wind. I hurried into the dark, shoutin all the while, and the shooters, for it was them, of course, they shouted back. I came across them, oh, a mile or mair doon the glen, stumblin in the bog up to their knees, and in a terrible state. Sandy Murray's brother had done in his ankle and was leanin heavily on Sandy Murray's cousin, who looked fit to drap and was screamin wi the cramp in his legs.

'We got lost,' said he and I telt him to wheesht and save his energy. I got in the middle of the twa of them and they wrapped themsels ower my shoulders and I dragged them up the hill to the bothy. Thon was the hardest half hoor of my life, even yet I think it was and I've kent hardships in my time, but I got them there all the same, and plonked them onto the heather and set to wi the kettle on the fire.

'Man,' said Sandy Murray's brother, 'I thocht we were done for.' I busied mysel pourin the tea. I didnae say so, but so had I, juist for a moment, when I was lyin in thon heather bed listenin to the sounds of my mind afore reason took hold and explained to me what was what in the world.

'Aye so,' said I, 'you're safe and weel noo, and nae harm done, save a sprained ankle and some weary banes.'

We drank oor tea and there was too much fatigue in that wee bothy for conversation, so I settled doon in the chair by the fire, leavin the heather bed for the shooters, and the three of us fell quickly to sleep. And aye, I dreamed of Aisling Campbell, but hae I no done the same every single nicht these past fifty year? I woke up next mornin wonderin aboot thon door, how it managed to shut and lock itsel. There would be an explanation for it, richt enough, juist as there was an explanation for the Big Grey Man on the mountain earlier and for thon ghostly voice in the nicht, somethin fae the world if I juist thocht aboot it long enough. And, mair difficult than them even, there would be an explanation for what I did to Aisling Campbell. Aye, and I still believe that today, even though fifty year has passed and I'm no closer to kennin the truth of it. There's nae need to hurry the thinkin, after all. It's no as if I'm goin ony place.

Man Walks Into A Bar

This isn't easy to say.
Schadenfreude.
Bless you.
Haha.
I'm afraid I have some bad news, Mr Orion.
No news is good news.
This is very difficult.
Like trigonometry? That was ay Greek to me too.
We can offer palliative care. It may give a few months extra. I'm sorry.
Close the door, walk away. Good time guy gone for a burton. Never a day sick in my life. Except my wedding night, right enough, sick as a budgie that night. Boom boom.
So here's me. There's that. I'm speechless, numb. It wasnae meant to be this way. What's that? A joke? I'll tell you a joke. There's this guy walks into a bar. No, this gorilla walks into a bar, lights up a cigarette. No, sorry, there's a punchline here somewhere. Give me a minute.
A minute? Jesus.
Forty-three years. Is that all I get?
There's this guy driving down the M62 when Helen phones his mobile. 'Stuart, be careful. I heard on the news there's someone driving the wrong way down the motorway.'
'Helen,' says Stuart, 'it's not just one, there's hundreds of the buggers.'
Did I say my name?
Yes. Stuart.

Two elephants walk off a cliff. Boom boom.
What d'you call a fish with no eyes?
A fsh.
What d'you call a man with only months to live?
What?
Skeleton walks into a bar. Says 'bartender, gimme a beer and a mop.'
Sidesplitter, huh?
Blind man walks into a wall.
Okay, tasteless.
Horse walks into a bar. Barman says 'why the long face?'
Stuart Orion walks into a bar.
Barman says 'why the long face?'
A skeleton, a horse and a Scotsman walk into a bar. Barman says 'what's this? A fucking joke?'
That's what I said to the doctor, too.
He wasnae laughing either.

The White Deer

Calum McAlpine, son of farmer Michael and his wife Mary, went into Crieff carrying the last of the family's money with the intention of buying flour and potatoes and meat for the winter. Instead, he spent it on ale. The next afternoon, as he was walking sore-headed and hungry by the banks of the Earn, oblivious of the unseelie court around him, he espied a deer. It was a white deer, a female, standing across the river and watching him. Its neck was long and slender, haunches muscular, tail raised, ears twitching. It seemed to shimmer in the dull light of the day. He raised his shotgun and trained his sights on the beast. The deer did not flinch. It did not run. It watched Calum with tranquil beauty. Calum, hungry as death, felt for the trigger of his shotgun and prepared to fire.

'Come to me,' the deer said.

Calum lowered his shotgun. 'I cannot swim,' he replied.

'And I cannot speak, yet you hear me anyway.'

Calum nodded and he pulled off his boots and his trousers and his shirt and he plunged naked into the cold of the River Earn. The current was strong but so was he and they battled, the river and the man, like lovers bickering, like warriors fighting unto friendship, and gradually the man prevailed, beat the current, crossed the water, made the bank. The white deer's black eyes watched him.

'Summer is nearly over,' she said. 'And your harvest is poor.'

'It is, aye. Too much rain and scant sun.'

'And you have spent all your money.'

'Aye. And nothin to show for it.'
'You and your family will not survive the winter, perhaps.'
'That's possible.'
'I can help you.'
'You can?'
'But only you.'
'Why only me?'
'You are the only one with the ambition to understand.'

The deer settled on her side, kicking her legs. She was old, Calum thought, unlikely to see out winter herself, and yet she was still striking in her elegance. Every movement was poetic, the shiver of her haunches, the quiver of her belly. Her teats were heavy.

'Drink,' she said. 'And if you drink this milk you will never grow hungry again.'

Calum had not eaten for a day or more and his stomach was cramping for want of food. There was nothing at home. He had spent all their money. He knew he should refuse but he knew he would not.

He got to his knees and bent towards the white deer, smelling her odour, the animal power of her scent. He took a teat and started to suckle and her warm liquid filled his stomach. He suckled and suckled, transfixed by the taste in his mouth, like nothing he had ever known. It was fresh and strong, musky, like sweet cicely and cinnamon, like molasses and lime, and the sensation of it sliding down his throat, viscous, almost alive, was a sensual, almost sexual pleasure.

'Enough,' said the white deer.

'No,' replied Calum. 'I need more.'

'Enough,' she said again but she did not insist. She watched him, watched as he guzzled, as his belly filled, as his body gorged, as his ambition grew sated.

When finally he stopped the white deer got to her feet. She was sleek, her skin taut, muscles tight. She looked younger, like an animal in the prime of her life. Her eyes shone. She bucked her head and ran off into the woods behind the railway line, sliding unerringly between a tightness of trees and into the dark.

And then she was gone.

Calum watched for an hour or more and the trees shook and the grass waved but no further movement came. He felt a loneliness then that was as wide as the world and as cold as the moon and as dense as December skies. He headed for home, his stomach full, his soul empty. The journey was a hard one and by the time he reached the narrow path to his weary farm he was so tired it was an effort not to abandon himself by the roadside.

'Oh,' he thought. 'What hae I done?'

He entered a faded kailyard, silent in the afternoon, no sun nor warmth nor hospitality. He sought his parents, shouted into the cottage to them from the yard but, instead of his mother, an ancient hag appeared at the front door. Her hair was white and falling out in clumps. She had no teeth. Her skin was the colour of rabbit hide.

'Wha are you?' said Calum.

'What do you mean?' said the hag.

'Whaur is my mither? Whaur is my faither?'

'What's up with you, Calum?' said a voice from behind him and Calum turned to find a wizened old man, bent double and feeble, holding an axe like it was the weight of gold.

Calum looked at his parents, for he knew they were them, the hag and the wizened old man.

'What hae I done?' he said. 'What hae I done?'

'Did you only look efter yoursel?' said his mother the hag.

'No,' said the son.

'Did you think of your parents?' said his father the fossil.

'Of course,' said the son.

'Then there is nothing to fear,' said his mother. And

they shuffled towards him, the husks of his parents, arms outstretched in love and hope, holding all the memory of their remembered years.

But they saw, both of them together, the way the young man flinched, the way he stepped backwards, his defensive demeanour, blank disbelief.

'You turn us awa,' said his mother the hag and she shook her head as he denied it.

'You would hae us leave,' said his father the fossil and again the son demurred and again they recognised his lie.

'Tell me you love me,' said his mother.

'Tell me you love me,' said his father.

'I love you,' said Calum to the air, to the ground, to the cottage behind them. 'I love you. Is that no enough?'

'Words are never enough, son,' said his mother the hag. 'Words are only shapes in the air unless they hae meanin and they hae honour and truth.'

'Your words hae no shape,' said his father the fossil. 'Your words hae no meanin or honour or truth.'

Calum thought to argue but his belly was full and his eyes were weary and he knew that he needed to sleep. A good night's rest, he thought, and in the morning I shall be grand. He thought of the white deer, then, of her beautiful shape, the sheen of her skin, the ripple of muscle, the dark of her eyes. He felt a moment of loss, a melancholy sense of the end of it all. Ambition lost. He looked up at his bedroom window and pictured the bed in the corner and pictured himself within it but he knew he had no energy to climb the stairs or to undress or to clamber beneath the blankets. Instead he sank to the ground in the middle of the yard and settled himself and rested his head on his hands as though imperious in a four-poster bed.

'I wish to sleep,' he said but his eyes remained open and he knew he could not and he knew he would never sleep again.

Calum's father and Calum's mother, the farmer and his wife, Michael and Mary, they held hands in disappointment and despair.

'I always suspected,' said his mother, 'but I chose no to believe.'

'I always kent,' said his father, 'that your love was your ain. You love only yoursel.'

His mother bent over him, her bones in pain, her muscles cramping. 'I love you, son,' she said and she kissed his forehead once, a lingering kiss, and as she did so she turned into a white deer. She looked around for an instant and ran, fine and firm-legged, into the woods.

His father bent over him, his back in spasm, arthritic hands convulsing. 'I love you, son,' he said and he kissed his forehead once, a lingering kiss, and as he did so he turned into a white deer. He looked around for an instant. Ahead, in the woods, he saw his wife the deer standing and watching and waiting. He ran towards her and they disappeared, lovers in love, into the safety of the darkness of the woods.

And sixty years passed and for sixty years Calum the farmer, the son who knew no love but of himself, dinnered each day on a single blade of grass. His stomach, bloated still from the milk of the white deer, could accommodate no more. On his farm he grew no crops. He grew grasses and heathers, a steady turn of saplings, replaced each year before they could mature. He watched as his herd of deer grew, year on year, his brothers and sisters and nephews and nieces and wondered how ever he could feed them all. The weight of his work bore down on him heavier with every passing year.

In the distance, every night, he could hear the calm, deep bellow of a faraway deer. It may have been the white deer, it may have been his mother, it may have been his father. Calum never knew but he sang in his head a paean to each, in the hope that one of them might one day return.

Then, and only then, would he know how to love.

The Woman Who Called Herself Karen

Instead of turning down Galvelmore Street, Mally Vogel followed the Comrie road round the bends, out of town. Every step increased the distance between him and home. Thirty minutes after pub closing time, there was little traffic on the road, a couple of cars driving so slowly the drivers must surely be drunk, a William Low's lorry heading for Crianlarich, a young man on a bike without lights. Trees swayed in an insistent April wind. Something rustled in the undergrowth at Barnkittock but otherwise there was no sound. Mally swigged from a half bottle of Bell's and staggered through the ornate iron gates of the top park onto a path that meandered downhill towards the cafe and the shelter sheds.

'You can all go fuck yourselves,' he shouted into the night.

'Charming.'

Mally stopped. 'Who's there?' he said.

A woman appeared from the shadows of the shelter shed, clicking on high heels. Her hair was bird's-nested in a style from the early eighties. She wore a short coat above a shorter dress.

'I'm not interested, love,' said Mally.

'I'm not selling,' she replied. 'Done for the night.'

'You and me both.'

'Yeah, you look rough. I'd guess you drink too much.'

'And I'd guess you fuck too much.'

'Maybe. But when I get home I'll wash myself clean like it never happened. Tomorrow's a new day. What's tomorrow morning going to be like for you, with your hangover and your rage?'

'Who said I'm raging?'

'Who said "You can all go fuck yourselves"?'

The shadows observed one another, their movements obscured by blackness. Seconds passed. 'I'm Steve,' said Mally.

'You can call me Karen.' Without waiting, she walked on, past the tennis courts, the trampolines, disused paddling pool, roundabout, tall chute that was dangerously decaying but not yet condemned. Mally followed. At the entrance to the middle park there was a single sodium light, dimly orange, and they studied one another in silence. She was younger than Mally had imagined. No great looker.

'So what you doing out here in the middle of the night?' she said.

'Couldn't face going home.' Her being a prostitute made confession easier. She was indifferent. Wouldn't care what anyone told her. Probably heard stories like this every night from men exactly like Mally. She would tune them out, smile and stroke their cheeks and, for an hour anyway, help them forget the bleakness of their existence.

'Right,' she said. When they reached the park-keeper's hut the exit was to their left. They walked straight on, past giant pines and beeches downhill to the wooden bridge over the river Barvick and into the bottom park. Here, in a bowl surrounded by trees and sheer banking and the pulsing river, darkness was almost unconditional. At the last moment a row of swings materialised and they both stopped. The swings rocked as though being launched by the ghosts of the night. Mally and the woman who called herself Karen each took one and sat facing a river they could hear but not see. A car climbed the Laggan Hill but otherwise there was no sign of life.

'So what's at home?' she said. 'What's so bad you have to come here instead?'

'The wreckage of my life.'

'Melodramatic.'

'Truthful.'

'Explain.'

'Wife. Two kids. Boy and girl. Eleven and seven.'

'That doesn't sound so bad.'

'Failure.'

'Well, you know what Beckett said.'

'Who?'

'Samuel Beckett. "Fail. Try Again. Fail again. Fail better."'

'Bollocks.'

'Why?'

'As my mother used to say, "What's for you will no go past you".'

'What does that mean?'

'We're all fucked up. We just don't know it yet.'

'Everyone has the right to fuck up. But you don't have the right to give up.'

'Who says I have?'

'An eleven-year-old and a seven-year-old who didn't see their daddy tonight.'

He stared at her outline. 'That was cruel.'

'So's sitting in the park drunk as a skunk instead of going home to your family.'

He unscrewed the bottle of Bell's and took a mouthful. Acid spiked his gut. He offered her the bottle. She declined.

'Been in the pub tonight?' she said.

'Yeah.'

'And now a half bottle of whisky?'

'Yeah.'

'On your own.'

'Apart from you.'

'I don't count.'

'Why?'

'Because come morning you won't even know whether I was real or a figment of your imagination.'

'I'll remember.' But Mally knew she was right. He wasn't even sure now. He pinched the back of his hand and it didn't hurt. He pinched his cheek. When had he last felt physical pain? That part of him no longer existed.

'Give me a push,' said the woman. 'I want to fly.'

Mally stepped listlessly from his swing and positioned himself behind her. He could only vaguely make out her shape and he reached forward and pushed and she swung away. He pushed again, more firmly, and then again, and again, stepping back each time as her arc stretched higher with each passage.

'More,' she said.

After a couple of minutes, her backward swing was reaching the height of Mally's face. He saw nothing and then, at the last moment, the darkness shifted and there she was and he reached out and pushed her. His hand on her arse. He could feel it through her thin coat. Nice. He waited. A ripple in the night and there she was again. If he didn't concentrate, the back of her swing would hit him in the face. He concentrated. Watched. Waited. Pushed her arse, his fingers splayed for maximum contact. She flew higher and by now he had to stretch his arms to reach her. He grabbed the back of her seat and rose with it, feet off the ground, then pushed again. And she disappeared into the void again. Wait. Swish. Push. She was flying so high he could hear the chains of the swing slacken at the top of the arc as they lost tension.

'Higher,' she shouted.

But he stepped away and sat on his own swing again and waited as hers slowed and she skidded her feet on the ground until finally she came to rest and all that could be heard was

Mally's heavy breathing. His hands were still warm where he'd touched her. He ran them over his face.

'I haven't gone that high since school,' she said. 'I couldn't see anything. It felt like I was going round and round, not up and down. Like a rollercoaster.'

Mally lit a cigarette. He studied her profile in the light of the match. 'So what about you?' he said. 'Kids?'

'Shona. Seven.'

'Same age as my lassie. They're probably in the same class.'

'No, they won't be.'

'Why, are you Catholic?'

'No.'

'Then they probably are. Miss Malcolm's class. Primary Two.'

'She doesn't go to school in Crieff.' The woman who called herself Karen spoke quietly. She gripped the iron chain of the swing and pressed her cheek to it. It smelled like blood. She twisted her head until the chain was against her throat. She pushed until it hurt.

'Who's looking after her now? Sheena?'

'Shona.'

'Who's looking after her?'

She stared in the direction of her feet. The Sandeman Library, Perth, once a week, Saturday mornings, always with that woman with the moustache and garlic breath. Saturday mornings, three hours in which to cram a week's love. Chaperoned while you met your own daughter, as if you'd do anything to hurt her. Three hours for Shona to talk about the new words she's learned and how she can do multiplication and how she has a party at Linda's tonight and she's got a new frock to wear for it. Three hours to tell Shona you love her and you love her and you love her.

'I don't really want to talk about it.'

Mally found her voice attractive. A young woman's voice

without the coarseness of age. His wife's voice was coarse. Cigarette rough. Quarrelsome. Castigating. He swigged from the whisky bottle again.

'Talk about something else, then,' he said.
'What?'
'Anything. Something nice.'

Something nice. The woman who called herself Karen would have to delve into her history for that. The trouble with having no family was that there were no events to share, no memories to log. There were no trig points in the landscape of your life with which to map your progress. No-one to kiss. No-one to love. Except Shona. No-one to love.

'She doesn't live with me.'
'Who?'
'Shona.'
'Why not?'

Because your behaviour is putting your daughter at risk. It's not a safe environment for a child. Neglect. It's in her best interests, you must understand. You'll still be able to see her. Escorted.

She gripped the swing so tightly it hurt. This was what her life comprised. A cold swing in the biting dark. An empty house with an empty bedroom with an empty bed. Empty mornings and empty nights.

'Why not?'
'She was taken into care.'
'Why? Cos you're a hooker?'

'I'm not really a prostitute. I just do it sometimes to pay the bills. End of the month.' A pulse throbbed in her ear. Cold was seeping up her legs. Night bore down on her. 'When they took Shona into care I wasn't in control. I had debts. I couldn't cope. That was eight months ago.' *Eight months without my baby. Eight months on my own.* 'I'm so, so lonely.'

Mally took a final drag of his cigarette and threw it onto

the grass. It hissed and extinguished and they were returned to invisibility.

'Me too,' he said.

'You've got a wife.'

'We never talk. Never even look at each other. I haven't had a fuck in months.'

'Me neither.'

'But...'

'They don't count. It isn't me does that. It's someone else. I'm not even there.'

Mally knew about that. About going through the motions. He did it every waking moment. He reached across and felt for her hand. She didn't react. 'Can we fuck?' he said.

'No.'

'It wouldn't be you. It'd be someone else.'

'No.' She closed her eyes. She tried to picture Shona but her daughter wasn't there. She was in a bed in a house in a town seventeen miles away and the woman called Karen had been told she had no right to be with her. She knew that. She would never accept it.

'I'll pay.'

'I told you, I'm not a prostitute.'

'Okay, I won't pay.'

'No.'

'A blowjob?' Wind whistled through the trees. The river ran. Mally looked into the blackness. Then he heard her crying. She cried for some moments and it wasn't gentle. It was the sound of agony. Failure engulfed them both.

'Okay,' she said.

When they were done, she spat his semen onto the grass and sniffed loudly and wiped her nose on her coat sleeve. They lapsed into silence. Mally lit another cigarette. 'I'm not really called Steve,' he said. 'I'm Mally.' She didn't reply. 'You're not called Karen either, are you?'

'No.'

'What's your real name?'

The woman who called herself Karen stood and started to walk across the grass to the bridge, the road, to home, to bed. She turned and in the darkness she gave Mally Vogel a wave he couldn't see.

'That's too personal,' she said.

She crossed the bridge and walked away.

Taking Tea With The Other Woman

I'm sitting, as is now my custom, taking tea with the other woman. I don't like it but there's nothing I can do, so tea it is, with the other woman politely by my side and gentle conversations gradually weaving a new and horrible history.

It started last December when Peter and I were watching a DVD. The programme was *The Lost World of Frieze-Green* and in it two 1920s girls were sashaying down the street towards the camera. I was reaching for my wine when Peter turned rigid beside me.

'What?' I said.

'That's me.'

'What is?'

'The girl on the left.' He paused the frame. A woman, pretty, vaguely familiar, filled the screen. She had a shapeless hat and choppy hair. Her nose was long and her smile was broad.

'That's me.'

'What are you talking about?'

He gripped my hand. He couldn't take his eyes from the screen.

'Marjory Compton,' he said. 'My name is Marjory Compton. I'm nineteen and this is my friend Valerie. We're going into town to buy stockings for the dance in the town hall.'

'Very funny.'

'My God, it's like a door's opened in my memory.' He was shaking so hard his wine sloshed from the glass. He gabbled some nonsense about his 'family' – mother dead, father a drunk, servant called Emily – and their house in the country and how he was engaged to John de Coursey.

The pause button's cut-out kicked in and the programme started again.

'The girl on the left is called Marjory Compton,' the commentary said. *'She was on her way to buy stockings for a dance.'*

'Is this a joke? Have you seen this before?'

'I don't need to. I'm telling you, this is me.'

I switched off the DVD and flounced into the kitchen.

The programme became one of those forbidden subjects. Peter tried to talk but I wouldn't let him. It had been a symptom of stress, I supposed. He was working too hard. We took a holiday in the Seychelles and he was fun, like the Peter I fell in love with ten years ago. He stopped mentioning Marjory Compton. I forgot about her.

I found him watching it one weekend when I was supposed to be out with the girls but came home because I'd a headache. I'd thrown the DVD out after that night, so he must have bought another copy. He was watching it in slow-motion, smiling. Anger kicked in.

'Here we go again!'

'You don't understand.'

'Too bloody right. Your name is Peter MacKintosh. You are not Marjory Whatever-her-fucking-name is. Do – you – understand?' I was embarrassed to be so jealous of a long-dead woman but I couldn't change the truth. 'I never want to see this shit again.'

He nodded but I knew he was lying.

I checked his internet history. He had been searching for Marjory Compton everywhere. Family-tree sites, local history groups, chatrooms. I cried as I waded through it all. I felt Peter's hand on my shoulder. He handed me a portfolio.

'This is me,' he said. 'You have to understand.'

There were pages and pages of notes, the history of Marjory Compton. There were pictures of her, one in a long, elaborate christening gown, another as a teenager smiling coyly at the camera. I had to admit, there was a resemblance.

'I don't like this either,' he said. 'But it's there.'

A few weeks later I brought him a cup of tea one Saturday afternoon.

'Who are you?' he said. His voice was different, lilting. I looked into his eyes but he wasn't there. I started to cry.

It was me who bought him his first dress. I knew he wanted it. It was a fine Edwardian tea gown, and we bought embroidered stockings too, and a picture hat. It was a month before we could find a suitable corset. His shoes were bespoke.

When he comes home at night I take his hand and lead him to the bedroom. I undress him and wash him, clean away the grime of modernity. I help him into his corset and stockings and white gown. I sit him on the bed and slip his feet into his shoes.

'Thank you, Emily,' he says. 'Do you think Mr de Coursey will call today?'

'I'm sure he will, ma'am,' I reply.

I go downstairs and prepare to make tea. The other woman follows in her finery.

Not Drowning Yet

Carmela Cant stared at a greyness of sky. She pulled back her head until it was under water and the noise of the world was muted except for rain pulsing on the surface of the reservoir. She flicked her hands and glided a few feet further from the edge. She wore only underwear and the cold had moved beyond painful to become a delicious numbness. It felt as though she had no body. Her mind could follow.

A crow flew past, intruder breaking the grey. Another. Carmela closed her eyes to banish them and drifted in darkness material. She submerged her head again and opened her eyes. The water's surface was above her and beyond was nothing, a void in time and memory and pain, world ambivalent. She wanted to sink, uncouple herself, escape. This feeling, this feeling of nothingness, let it come, let me go. But suddenly there was a flash across the meniscus and a face was staring down, eyes wide as a madman, mouth open, shouting. She tried to scream and swallowed a mouthful of water. Pain exploded in the back of her head and she gulped again and swallowed water again and sank back, twisting and turning out of control. She rose, breaking the surface.

'I've got you.'

The water was churning as though alive. It's claiming me, she thought, before she understood that human hands were clutching her, not Death's, and she realised there was a boy there. He tried to wrap his arm around her but missed and punched her jaw.

'I've got you,' he repeated but the more he tried to help

the more he dragged Carmela down. And, as she fell beneath the surface, so did he.

'Stop it,' she shouted. She gripped his shoulder but he tried to break free. There was terror in his eyes. He sank again and swallowed water and snorted it out of his nose and thrashed impotently. Carmela hooked her arm across his chest and felt him relax. She struck out and began to swim across the reservoir with one arm, holding onto the boy with the other. By the time they reached the reservoir's edge the boy was sobbing and Carmela's shoulders were aching. She heaved herself out of the water and reached and pulled the boy onto the bank.

'What the fuck were you doing?' she said.

'Saving you.'

'You nearly fucking killed me.'

'I'm sorry.'

She wrapped herself in her duffle coat and sat on the bank and pulled up her knees and shivered. 'Cover yourself up,' she said, turning away from his scrawny body.

He wiped himself dry with his grey school shirt and pulled on his trousers and fastened his jacket. 'I'm Kenny,' he said.

'I know.'

'You're Carmela.'

'I know that, too.'

'I'm in your wee sister's year at school.'

'Jesus, stop telling me things I already fucking know. What are you doing here, anyway? Why aren't you in school?'

'I could ask you the same question.'

'Cos I'm a fucking nutcase. Miss Crazy, 1980.'

'You're not a nutcase.'

'Carmela the loony.'

Kenny didn't reply. Carmela had a reputation in school for being strange but full loony status had only been conferred the week before, when she dragged a piano into her front garden in Maxton Road and played *The Entertainer* on it naked. Madwoman on the rampage. Carmela Cant Crazy Cunt. Kenny McAskill had been one of the crowd who watched the performance. Unlike the rest, he hadn't laughed.

'You don't have to be polite,' she said. 'I know what people say about me. I don't give a fuck.'

Kenny didn't know how to answer. 'That's the best way,' he said.

They sat in silence, Carmela rocking back and forwards in irritation at Kenny's presence. Kenny didn't dare look at her. Finally, Carmela spoke. 'Maria reckons you've got a crush on me. Is that right, wee Kenny?'

'Aye.' He spoke so softly it was barely more than a breath. Carmela looked up in surprise. She had expected denial, embarrassment, anger. She had wanted to unsettle him.

'Well, you've no fucking chance,' she said.

'I know.'

'Find someone your own age.'

'You're only two years older than me.'

'Find someone who's not a nutcase.'

'Stop calling yourself that.'

'It's true.'

'It's not.'

'I dream of death. That nutty enough for you?'

'So do I.'

'Sure you do.'

'I do.'

Carmela felt her irritation grow. The kid was giving all the wrong answers. She wanted to get angry and he was being too fucking reasonable. 'Alright,' she said. 'Tell me. Tell me about your dreams of death.' He didn't answer and she prodded him. 'You see? Liar. You're just saying that. Trying to ingratiate yourself. Bastard.'

But Kenny had never spoken of this before, not to

anyone, and the telling wasn't easy. He took a breath. 'I get this dream every other night, more or less.' He looked up as a crow scored across the low sky. It wheeled and turned west. 'The Highlandman's Loan. You know it?'

'Yeah.'

'Between the Gilmerton bends and Duchlage.'

'For fuck's sake, stop telling me things I know.'

'D'you know why it's called the Highlandman's Loan?'

'No.'

'It was the route Bonnie Prince Charlie's troops took when they marched towards Crieff during the Jacobite rebellion.'

'Fascinating.'

'I know it isn't. But anyway, when I was in primary school I was obsessed by it. The whole Jacobite thing. I still am. So in my dream I'm at the foot of the Highlandman's Loan. And I can hear it in the distance, pipers playing *Scotland the Brave*. And then I see them rounding the bend a mile uphill, a battalion of Jacobite warriors marching towards me, coming closer, closer. And then, when they're about half a mile away, I see that they're marching backwards. I can't make sense of it at first, but then I see their plaids billowing behind them and rucking around their bodies, and they're not marching at all. It's more of a shamble. Their step is all unsteady and uneven, and the pipes are out of tune and there's no rhythm. And as they get closer I start to get this smell in my nostrils, like something that's been dead in a ditch a long time. And then they pass me, one by one, my Jacobite heroes. And they turn and stare at me. Some have got missing hands, arms, eyes. Stomachs gaping open. They're all bleeding and the blood is so red against their grey skin. They're moaning. Shaking their heads at me. Hundreds of them. Thousands maybe. And I watch them pass by and carry on down to Duchlage. The last one is a wee boy, my age. I try to shake his hand but he won't let me. 'You didn't see anything,' he says. 'We're not here.' Then he follows the battalion and once they're past me they turn into a cloud and the cloud hovers over the earth and it starts to rain blood and it covers everything. Me included. And then I wake up.'

Carmela stared at him, this solemn-faced boy. He wouldn't make eye contact, just gazed straight ahead, across the reservoir. She could tell he was waiting for a reaction.

'Jesus, you're as fucked up as me.'

'Thank you.'

'Why? Why do you dream that?'

'I don't know. Dad used to say I've got an over-active imagination.'

'You think stuff like that a lot?'

'Yeah.'

'D'you write it all down?'

'Yeah.'

She stood up. 'I knew you were a writer. That story of yours in the school magazine last term. Was that about me?'

'I was really, really angry about that. They should have asked my permission before printing that.'

'But was it about me?'

'Not really.'

'Cos if it was it's rubbish. You don't know anything about the way girls think.'

'I know. That's why they shouldn't have printed it.'

'What's a boy doing writing stories about a girl anyway? "A Depressed Teenager". Jesus, a girl runs away from home and before she gets half a mile she regrets it and runs all the way back again and shouts for her mummy. That's just shit. Why would you write that?'

'Because I wanted a happy ending.'

She snorted. 'Life's not like that.'

'I know. But I'd like it to be.'

She took off her coat and picked up her blouse and put it on and buttoned it. 'Show's over,' she said. She reached for her skirt.

He tried not to look at her panties, the crinkle of pubic hair beneath. It was the most erotic thing he'd ever seen. 'It was nice,' he mumbled. He turned and studied the grass between his legs.

She laughed. 'You're a very strange boy, Kenny McAskill.'

'So I'm told.'

She fastened her skirt and pulled on her socks and shoes. Kenny was fourteen but looked younger. His body was hairless, she had noticed earlier. He was intense, lonely. His eyes were the same as hers when she looked in the mirror. Defensive. Defenceless. She sat down again.

'Do you get bullied?' she said.

'Not really. I don't mix with the other boys much. I prefer girls, to be honest, but they don't speak to me.'

'Why do you prefer girls?'

'You're more interesting. None of that macho stuff.'

'Are you a poof?'

'No.'

'I think you are. You maybe don't know it yet.'

'If I was a poof why would I fancy you?'

'Because I'm more of a boy than a girl.'

'No you're not. You're beautiful.'

'I'm not talking about my looks. And no I'm not. It's the way I think that's like a boy.'

'How?'

'Boys think literally. Boys are aggressive.'

'You're not like that.'

'I fucking am.'

'You aren't.'

'So what am I like then, shrimp?'

'Bright. Funny. Unhappy.'

'One out of three right.'

'Which one?'

'Ha ha ha.' Carmela lit an Embassy Regal and exhaled noisily, leaning her arms on raised knees. She offered the pack to Kenny and he took one and put it in his mouth as Carmela flicked the lighter. He rested his hand on hers and felt a frisson as they touched. He inhaled deeply and immediately started to cough and he tried to cover it up by inhaling again. A cold sweat washed over his brow and he felt instantly dizzy, the coughing by now uncontrollable. He tried to focus on the water ahead of him but it was shifting. The cigarette shook in his hand.

'You don't smoke?' said Carmela, staring at him with a bemused expression.

'No.'

'What did you take one for, then?'

'Cos you offered me it.'

She shook her head. 'Give me it.' She grabbed the cigarette and picked off the embers and pushed the stub back into her packet. 'You don't have to do what people tell you, you know. Do what you want.'

'Okay.'

They sat in silence while Carmela finished her cigarette and Kenny's mind churned through the humiliation of trying to be mature and failing. There was an acrid taste in the back of his throat and the dizziness hadn't cleared and he thought he might be sick. It took some minutes to pass.

'Thanks for trying to save me.'

'That's okay.'

'Just, don't do it again.' He looked as though he was about to object. 'Seriously. You nearly killed us both.'

He laughed. Carmela laughed. She sat back and rested her weight on her palms. Kenny copied her pose and they each stared up at a sky that was the colour of a week-old bruise.

'Were you really?' Kenny said. 'Going to kill yourself?'

Carmela pondered for a moment. 'No.'

'I'm glad.'

'But I will. One day.'

'Please don't.'

'It's not really up to you, is it?'

'All the same.'

'It's not up to me either, to be honest. I'm not going to do it now. Not this year. Next year, even. But one day, I know it'll happen. It'll get too much and I'll just disappear. Everyone will be looking for me. Search parties, the lot. Except you. You'll know I'm here. But you won't tell anyone.' She turned to him. 'You'll leave me in peace, won't you, Kenny? Because it's what I want?'

'But it's a reservoir.'

'So?'

'So you'll poison the town's water supply.'

Carmela laughed. 'Good. People think I'm poison anyway. It'll be funny to prove them right.'

'It's not funny.'

'It's not serious, either.'

'It is. It'd be tragic.'

'Bollocks. If I was happy, if everyone loved me, if I was popular and beautiful and clever, but then I got cancer and died, or I fell under a bus, that would be tragic. But this is just crazy Carmela Cant realising enough's enough and deciding that sinking under the water and staying there forever is preferable to anything else the world has to offer. How can that be tragic?'

'But you can play the piano.'

'What the fuck's that got to do with anything?'

Kenny felt a wave of embarrassment as he saw the scorn in her expression. 'Sorry,' he said. 'I don't know. It just makes you real. Having a skill like that. The enjoyment it brings you. I think about the happiness you must feel when you sit down to play. That makes me want to smile.'

Carmela gripped his hand and held it tightly. 'I'm serious.

I'll do it anyway, some day, so it won't make any difference whether you tell anyone or not. I'll still be dead, either way. But thing is, when I am I just want to be left alone. I don't want to be found. Never. No funeral. No phonies. You understand?' She leaned forward and kissed him once on the lips and sat back and stared into his startled eyes.

'Promise me,' she said. 'Like the boy in your dream. Promise me you'll tell them you didn't see anything.'

Kenny looked up at the clouds, portent of more rain, dark inevitable. Blood rising. There were no crows. Nothing broke the grey. He felt suddenly grown up.

'You're not here,' he said.

She continued to stare at him, appraising him. 'You're just saying that, aren't you? Because you think it'll never happen. You won't have to do it.'

He paused, then nodded twice. 'Sorry.'

'I told you. There are no happy endings. Life's not like that.'

'It can be. If you do what you want.'

She gave a sickly smile. 'Nice try, kid. Come back in five years' time. See if you still think that.'

'I will. If you will.'

She shrugged. 'Who's to say?'

The Weight of Snow

First the hills disappeared, then the road through the valley, then Farmer MacKenzie's fields, and the hedges, and the trees. There was no sky, no ground. Just grey, like the world was dissolving. Dull. A dullness smothered the Strathearn valley. When people talk about the winter of nineteen sixty two and three they usually mean after January but, up in Perthshire, the snow started in November and forgot to stop and before long it was feet deep and the world was flattened into indistinction. The cold was a coarseness against your skin. Your nostrils froze.

'Heavens, will it never end?' I said.

Even Faither had never seen the like. 'If it goes on much longer we'll be stranded,' he said. It seemed to me we already were. It had been three days since Faither had been to Crieff or I had gone to school, but that wasn't stranded, he said. That was just being careful. 'We could get oot if we had to.'

The walls of the bothy, its low ceiling with a single, bare lightbulb, enveloped me. A pale fire smoked in the grate and Mum's picture hung above it, with the tarnished mirror alongside that no-one thought to look in, now. There were only the two chairs, either side of the fire. You could still see marks on the rug where a third had sat.

'Maybe we should try to get to toon?' I said.

'We'll be grand.'

'We havenae mony tatties left. Or ingins.'

'We'll be grand.'

I thought of Mum and started to cry. Stop it, Peggy, I

said to myself. I buttoned my coat and wrapped my scarf round my face and put on my gloves and opened the front door. Immediately, an alien coldness slithered beneath my clothing and wrapped itself around me. I could barely move. Breathing hurt. I dragged the ladder from the barn and propped it against the front of the bothy to sweep snow from the roof with a broom. As soon as I swept it clear the swirl of wind and snow turned it white again.

'For goodness sake, lassie, come inside. You'll get pneumonia.'

He was staring from the doorway with his sleeves rolled up and the top three buttons of his shirt undone. He hadn't shaved. Heaven knows what he was looking at for there was nothing to be seen, just snow, snow, snow. I went in to boil a kettle and it was ten days before I stepped outside again.

I was thirteen and this was our first Christmas without Mum. She took a fever in the middle of April and she said she was fine and she would work through it and she died on Easter Monday with a racking cough that rang through the bothy for hours until both it and she subsided into silence. I held her hand the night before and she smiled but Faither wouldn't allow me in the room when it happened and there is a hole in my existence now that can never be filled. It didn't help that Faither wouldn't speak of her afterwards. He sealed up his emotions and bore the weight of loss and lived less vigorously with each passing day. I knew he was in pain so I said nothing. Instead, I carefully curated every memory of her, terrified that I should forget a single moment.

Those first few days, snowfall and winds howling like wolves, we settled into a routine. The battery in the radio ran out so we had to make our own entertainment. I played my fiddle and we sat and talked and he taught me cards. After a while I could beat him at whist, and then at gin rummy. He could never remember what suit I was saving. There was no fire in my bedroom and getting ready for bed was a nightly torture. I was beginning to view the cold as an enemy and I hated baring myself to it. I asked Faither if there were any more blankets but there weren't. 'Sleep doonstairs,' he said.

'No,' I said. I was knitting him a scarf for his Christmas present with some grey wool from an old school sweater I'd grown out of. I was slow at the knitting, not like Mum, and I only had time to do a few rows each night before my fingers were too numb to hold the needles. Then I'd coorie under the blankets and try not to move and convince myself I was fine and warm. As Christmas Day approached I grew more excited and I felt guilty about that. And I worried, too, that I wouldn't finish the scarf in time. I didn't want to disappoint Faither. Not that first Christmas. So when I'd finished my knitting each night I would bury my head in my pillow and try to ignore the creaking roof and will myself to sleep.

All the while the snow kept falling and the world grew quieter. Icicles barred the windows and beyond them nothing was recognisable. Nothing moved. The icicles lengthened and snow reached the bottoms of the windows. We hadn't opened the front door for four days and Faither said that in a couple more we wouldn't be able to. All that existed were the two of us and our little bothy and our memories and my cold bed upstairs and the outside which seemed to be trying to push inside. The days passed.

'I'm just going upstairs, Faither,' I said on Christmas Eve afternoon.

'Dinnae be daft,' he said. 'It's ower cold up there.'

But I insisted. The scarf still wasn't finished. I pulled it from under my bed and untangled the wool. It wasn't a very grand affair, now that I looked at it in daylight, and I worried it wasn't as good as I'd hoped.

As I cast off a new row I became aware of the creaking again. It had kept me awake the night before, the rafters groaning like Faither's knees when he climbed the stairs, and in daylight the noise seemed louder than ever. The roof sometimes creaked in summer when the days were hot but I hadn't heard it in winter before.

'Shut up,' I shouted and started knitting. There was a hole near the bottom of the scarf where I'd dropped a stitch which I'd have to darn when I'd finished. I didn't want any more mistakes so I worked slowly, crouching, trying not to shiver. I knitted in time to the creaking of the roof and got a rhythm going and it helped me to finish another fifteen rows. I only had another six inches or so to do and I lay back in my bed and closed my eyes, picturing Faither opening it on Christmas morning. I hoped he might smile. Then came the loudest crack of all, like thunder, like the end of the world.

I sat up and I was immediately dizzy. There was something strange. The room seemed out of kilter, too big, too close. I stood up slowly, worrying that I might fall over. The shape of the roof was all wrong. It was bowed, bending in as though trying to grab me, and it was only now that I realised the creaking was not only louder but faster.

'Faither!' I yelled. 'Faither.' I rushed downstairs. Faither was sitting by the fire, staring into it. I ran for the door. 'The roof. The roof.'

When I opened the door there was a band of daylight at the top a couple of feet wide and the rest was snow.

'What can we do?' said Faither.

'The kitchen windae,' I said. 'It's on the ither side. The snow winnae be as deep.'

As we stood in front of the window it was obvious Faither wouldn't fit through it. 'It'll hae to be me,' I said. 'Help me up.' He lifted me too quickly and I scratched my shoulder against the largest of the icicles, knocking it loose. I punched out the others and steadied myself and jumped down and sank into the snow to my waist. The pain came after a few seconds, like my flesh was being flayed. 'Gie me the broom,' I said.

After so long indoors the brightness of the snow and the

clear blue sky hurt my eyes. Cold sliced at my face. My fingers were already numbing. The ladder was where I'd left it days before, half submerged, and I climbed half a dozen rungs, the broom waving drunkenly in my hand. I started to push at the snow on the roof but it was about three feet deep and dense and hard and it wouldn't budge.

I hacked it with a shovel, jabbing hard and fast. There was a brief groan and a section of guttering fell off. A second later, in virtual silence, a strip of snow about one yard wide began to shift, slowly building momentum until it slid like a monumental slab down the pitched roof onto the ground at the side of the bothy. It was almost beautiful. I stretched to my right and hammered at another section and it too gave way and I cheered. This was easy. I shifted the ladder and started to push at the area to my left but it was even more compacted and nothing could shift it. I stretched further and as I did so I heard a shiver and a sigh and the area of snow directly above me broke free. I didn't have time to scream before it was on me, a wash of snow so thick and heavy and cold it was like being hit by a sheet of metal. My ladder was thrown backwards and I went with it and I was momentarily aware of flying through the air. It took seconds but felt like hours and I finally crashed into the snow in the yard and was buried six feet deep.

I lay there, winded, looking up at the sky, the clear blue, the eternal. It was surprisingly warm in my cocoon and I laughed. I don't know why. There was complete silence, a silence I've never experienced before or since. It was seductive. I could have stayed there.

'Move,' I shouted. 'Move.' I shifted from side to side but the snow was penning me in and I couldn't get enough impetus. I began to panic and struggled, panting and screaming, until I managed to turn on my front, my face pressing into snow. I climbed onto my knees and drew on my dwindling reserves of energy and stood up and shook my head and looked around.

'Are you okay?' Faither was at the window, puffing at his pipe.

'Aye.' I picked up the ladder and looked for the shovel and broom and started again. By the time I'd finished the west-facing side I had worked out a routine and the snow on the east side was less compacted anyway so it shifted more easily. I finished in half an hour. Only then did I realise how cold I was. Faither wrapped a blanket around me and sat me on my seat by the fire. I didn't stop shivering until nightfall.

'Sleep by the fire,' he said. My body ached, my shoulder throbbed, my fingers still felt numb. I was tired and I wanted to close my eyes and sleep for days. Then I remembered the scarf.

'I'm fine,' I said and stood up but I was so shaky I fell back into the chair and when I woke up it was Christmas morning. The fire was dead in the grate and the only heat in the room was from the range, on which a kettle was boiling. Faither didn't seem to notice.

'Merry Christmas,' I said.

'Aye,' he said.

I heated yesterday's porridge and we sat and ate in silence as I replayed the events of the previous day. Faither should have known the weight of snow would damage the roof. He should have cleared it. Before Mum died he would have done. I was sure of that then and I'm sure of that now.

'Have we no more coal?' I said.

'Aye.' He swallowed a huge mouthful of porridge and spoke as he chewed. 'But no much.'

'How long afore we can get into toon?'

He shrugged. 'I dinnae ken. A week probably.'

After breakfast I inspected upstairs. The roof was still bowed, but not as much as before and I couldn't see light penetrating anywhere. With luck, there wouldn't be much damage. I pulled out the scarf and tied off the stitches and held it against the light of the window. It was too short and that hole was still there and the colour was desperately dull but there was nothing to be done. Folding it neatly, I went downstairs.

'For you,' I said. 'For Christmas.'

He took it in silence and spread it out. He brushed his hand across it and I noticed he had spotted the hole.

'That's braw,' he said. 'Just the thing for this weather.' He wrapped it round his neck and even though he didn't bother to knot it I could see it was plenty long enough after all. We looked at one another, waited. The waiting took on the stillness of confusion. Confusion gave way to embarrassment.

'I'm sorry, lassie. Wi the snow. Being stranded like this. I didnae hae time. I was goin to get you somethin last week.'

I looked out of the window. The snow had started again, whorling in the wind, obliterating the light. Mum smiled at me from her picture above the cold fireplace. The room seemed impossibly small and dark. Faither stood beside me with a drip hanging from his nose, not looking at me, not looking at anything, the grey scarf limp around his neck, and with sudden and absolute clarity I knew that for the rest of my life I would never forget this moment. Wherever I went, whenever it was, the memories of the past would drag me back to this place, this time.

This man.

I reached up and kissed his rough cheek.

'That's fine,' I said. 'We'll maybe get somethin in the January sales.'

'Aye, lass,' he said. He took off the scarf and laid it over his chair. 'Maybe.'

Oysters and Ink

1.

Emily picked up the phone three times and put it down again three times. She rehearsed her words. They sounded silly. Naive. They sounded like a young girl trying to act older. 'My folks have gone out. Wanna come round?'

What was hard about that?

She picked up the phone again. The circular dial recoiled slowly after each digit as though offering her time to think better of it. When she heard the ring tone it almost took her by surprise.

'Hello?'

She took a breath. 'Hi. It's me. My folks have gone out. Wanna come round?'

She'll say no. Silence, hellish silence.

'Gimme twenty minutes. Make myself beautiful.'

'More beautiful.'

'Ha!'

She rang off and Emily stared at the phone and wondered what she had done. No – not *done*, what she had *achieved*. Twenty minutes seemed like an hour. She wanted the doorbell to ring and she didn't. She did, she didn't.

The doorbell rang.

Ash was hunched into her jacket on the pavement when Emily answered. She gave Emily that wonderful cat-eyed smile and her blond hair swung about her shoulders. 'Hey,' she said and, as always, her American accent thrilled through

Emily. The sense of adventure it imbued, the freedom, that knowingness, so different from small-town Crieff, so assured, so relaxed.

'Upstairs,' said Emily and Ash passed into the hallway and led the way and Emily followed. 'First left,' Emily directed and without waiting Ash walked into her bedroom and flopped onto the bed. She looked round.

'Nice room. Bright.'

Emily looked at it as though for the first time. Posters on the wall. Bananarama. Wham. So childish.

'It'll do. Till I get a place of my own.'

'You lookin?'

Emily cursed. Every time she spoke it sounded gauche. 'Not yet,' she said. 'When I go to uni.' She took a tray from the table beneath her window and placed it on the bed by Ash and sat down beside her.

'Whatcha got?'

'Oysters.'

'Wow. Never had oysters.'

'You have now.' Emily opened one with a small knife and slid the knife under it and cut it from its shell. 'Lay back.'

Ash tilted her head and Emily poured the oyster into her mouth. Ash chewed, then swallowed. Her face was overtaken by an expression Emily couldn't fathom. Surprise? Disgust? Delight?

Ash swallowed again and opened her eyes wide. 'Amazin,' she said.

Emily laughed and sliced open another and slid it into her own mouth and swallowed. 'I love them.'

'Gimme another.'

They ate four apiece and lay back on the bed and stared at the ceiling. Emily sat up. 'Can I see your tattoos again? I think about them a lot.'

Ash unbuttoned her jeans and slid them off and lay on her stomach on the bed. Emily leaned over and rested her head on the American girl's thighs. The tattoos, one on each leg, were intricately patterned, a three-dimensional image of a zip rising from each ankle to the backs of her knees. The zips were open half way up her calves and it appeared that her skin was peeling away, revealing in *trompe l'oeil* perfection successive layers beneath, down to bone.

'They're beautiful,' said Emily. She stroked first one zip, then the other. She wanted to kiss them. 'I've never seen anything like them.'

Ash rolled onto her back. 'The guy that did it, he took a bit of persuadin. Said he'd never tattooed a woman before. Didn't want to. I said, aside from a few missin inches, our bodies is jes the same as yours so why wouldn't you?'

'I'd love to have something like that.'

'Well, maybe wait till you leave home, I reckon.'

'I can't wait.'

Ash turned onto her side and leaned on her shoulder, facing Emily. 'You set on goin to university?'

'I think so.'

'You know so. You gotta do it.'

'It's not that easy. No one in my family has ever gone.'

'So be the first. Cause trouble.'

'I want to. So much. But I want to be sure I'm doing it for the right reasons.' Ash gave her an *explain yourself gal* look and Emily smiled. 'Is it really because I want to go to uni, or just because I want to get away from Crieff?'

'Cain't it be both?'

Emily thought for a moment. 'My family's from Crieff. We've lived here for generations. That's why I sit in the graveyard to write my stories, beside their graves. I love the atmosphere. Especially early mornings. I feel like I can connect. I try to pick up their wisdom.'

'Ain't gonna get much wisdom outa that lot, honey. They long gone.'

'I don't mean it literally. It's the feeling they create. In me. They're my ancestors. I don't know that I want to lose that connection.'

'I never much got that feelin. Didn't even know my grandparents, none of em, so I guess I never felt close to no one. I never figured out how the pattern works. How it all fits together. You know? My whole life I ain't felt like I was from noplace. All I ever wanted was someplace to belong.'

'And all I've ever wanted was to escape.'

'Ain't that the way of it? We all want what we ain't got.'

Emily smiled ruefully at the thing she hadn't got. She slid up the bed and rested her head on the pillow next to her. 'You're very young to be without family,' she said. 'It must be hard.'

'Yeah. My daddy died six, seven years ago, so it was jes me and momma for a long time. And then she took cancer-sick ...'

'I've never known anyone die. Not in real life. Anyone close. Important.'

Ash rested her hand on Emily's waist. 'I wouldn't wish it on you,' she said. 'But you get on with it. One day passes, then another, then another. Each time it gets a mite easier to crawl out of bed in the mornin and back in again at night. The ghosts go away. Their noise hushes. Most times.'

'I'm sorry,' Emily said. 'It must be so hard. Family is important.'

'Yeah, so folks say. The fierce pull of blood. But is it? Really? What's so special about blood?'

'It's the best we've got?'

'It ain't much.'

'No.'

'Ain't love better?'

'I wouldn't know.'

'Me neither. Hey, let's fall in love. Find out.' They looked at each other and looked away. 'Where's them oysters,' Ash said when the silence had gone on too long. 'Gimme more.'

And Emily opened up another oyster and fed it to Ash and stared into her eyes and wondered if love was kindling.

2.

November 30th, 1984, the day her momma died, Ash hitched a ride into Richmond. There weren't any tattoo parlors in Berea and, besides, Richmond was the only town in Madison County licenced to sell alcohol. She lay on her stomach and reached for the tumbler of bourbon and winced at its sourness.

'You sure you wanna do this?'

'I said already.'

He drew the outline of the design she had given him on each leg in turn and wiped her skin with cleaning solution. The smell reminded Ash of the hospital she had walked out of three hours before. She closed her eyes. *Jes start. Make it hurt. Sorer'n hell.*

What he thought, this guy, was that he was tattooing a design onto Ash's skin. Ash knew otherwise. She knew he was bringing to the surface what was already in there. *What it is, is an excavation. Into me, Ash Harker, whoever she is. Somewhere inside me there's a real person, only I ain't found her yet.*

She already knew that by the time she was forty she would be tattooed from neck to toe, every centimetre of her body except her heart. That would remain untouched, untouchable. And each tattoo would represent the fault inside her and the pain she inflicted on everyone around her. They would be her mark.

The man switched on the tattoo gun and Ash smiled.

3.

The phone call surprised her. Emily wasn't usually one to initiate things. *Gal's too shy for her own good.* She looked at herself in the mirror. *Make myself beautiful. Hell, I ain't beautiful. Ordinary, everday pretty is all.* Not like Emily. She really was beautiful.

'Hey,' she said when Emily answered the door. She forced a smile. She walked inside. Family portraits hung on the walls, Emily through the years from toddler to school prefect, alongside doting parents, sometimes a flighty labrador, occasionally friends. The pattern of family life. Upstairs, she lay on Emily's bed and gazed at a room that was warm and bright and happy.

Homely.

Wouldn't that be somethin? A place to call home?

The oysters were like eating salted rubber. She thought she might gag and forced herself to swallow without breathing to minimise the taste. It was obvious Emily had been planning a special afternoon and Ash tried not to spoil it.

Cos ain't that what I do best?

'Amazin,' she said.

Emily fed her another, and another, and another, and despite their taste Ash thrilled at Emily's proximity, the feeling of the younger girl's breath on her cheek Close enough to kiss. She raised her hand to Emily's as though helping to steady it. Touch. Electricity. Afterwards, they lay side-by-side on the bed, the empty oyster shells discarded beside them and they talked and Ash wanted the afternoon never to end because she knew that when it did so would everything else.

'Can I see your tattoos again?'

Sure you can, jes don't go thinkin they're beautiful, cos they ain't.

'They're beautiful.'

Emily's head was resting on her thighs, hair tickling her skin. Ash lay still. Emily's pillow smelled fresh, pure. It smelled of Emily. Desire butterflied deep inside Ash. She could feel Emily tracing the marks of her tattoos with her fingers, first one zip, then the other. *Wipe them away, love, erase them, close up the scars and make me real.*

'My whole life I ain't felt like I was from noplace. All I ever wanted was someplace to belong.'

And this ain't the place, though I sure wish it was.

The girl from noplace had arrived in Crieff eight months before, cold, afraid, hopeful, newly orphaned and in search of the truth about her history. 'Just know that you are loved and were born of love.' That's what her momma told her before she died, that and the revelation that her daddy wasn't her real daddy. The girl she thought she was did not exist. The real Ash was waiting to be revealed. Maybe that version would be a better person?

'I met your real daddy in Scotland,' her mother said that final time in hospital before the morphine drifted her into obscurity. 'He was a good man. He would have loved you.'

Except he wasn't. He wouldn't. Ash had arrived in Scotland with $200 and the hope of a new existence but there was no father here. There was no family. Nothing to find, no trace, no pieces. Love was impossible for someone like Ash Harker. She was hollow. Empty. A hollow woman who left no trace and had no home and made no impression. A hollow woman with a hollow heart, failure inked on her skin like a portent.

'Hey, let's fall in love. Find out.'

See? See? You're snarin her now. Ash stared at Emily, her smiling eyes, her trusting expression, such affection, but there was too much noise in her head, so much confusion, the ghosts congregating, circling, plotting. Tomorrow, she would fly to Amsterdam. There were plenty tattoo parlours in Amsterdam. The design she would excavate from her spine was already inked in the notebook on top of her freshly packed rucksack. It was a snake.

Emily's room loomed over her, place of family, place of attachment. Place. At last, all the pieces, the whole pattern was known to her, and she had no part in it. The woman from noplace stroked Emily's shoulder and leaned up and kissed her. This once and nevermore. Her hand dropped and rested beside an empty oyster shell.

She stared into Emily's eyes and saw love extinguish.

Evanescence

Alison Disdain crouched in an over-large bath in the Station Hotel and looked at the whirlpool jets built into it and wondered how to make them work. The noise of an extractor fan drowned out the tinny radio by her bedside, from which John Timpson and Brian Redhead were presenting news of a day she didn't want to face. She stretched her legs and lay back and stared at the ceiling while long-repressed memories assailed her, shouting and anger, temper, contempt. Pictures from a different life. Her fearsome father looming over her. *Do this. Don't do that. My way the only way.* Alison closed her eyes. The water was too hot and her skin was turning pink. The stillness of it oppressed her. She agitated her hand beneath the surface and the sudden heat of the displaced water seared her breasts. Her leg stretched of its own accord, knee locking, foot arching. The foot turned inwards, toes sliding beneath the water. She wanted to do the same with her head, retreat from the present, but there wasn't enough water. She closed her eyes but the pictures remained. She hadn't felt like this in twenty years. She had forgotten what doubt felt like.

'Your name is Alison,' she said. 'Your name is Alison.'

*

An hour later, she put on a pair of jeans and a tee shirt. Then she took them off and looked at herself in the mirror. An exotic flower. Beauty frangible. Fear in a handful of hope. She selected a Laura Ashley dress, ridiculously flimsy given the rain falling ceaselessly outside. She put it on and felt human. By which she meant vulnerable.

At the undertakers, Danny Mills gave her the keys to her father's house. She slowly walked through Crieff, down King Street, along Commissioner Street, the Meadows, Burrell Street, Mill Street, Sauchie, Dallerie. *Litany. History.* Fear rose in her throat as every step took her closer to the past. Round the corner, down the brae, past the donkey field, on to the big house. Dallerie, home of Alistair Disdain and the Disdain family. Alistair, now Alison, the soft boy a perpetual disappointment to his bear of a father, the soft boy driven away, the woman now returned.

She stood at the front door for some moments as though unable to move. Then she unlocked it and swung it open and looked into the narrow hallway. Deer's head barometer on the right. It never worked. Perpetual promise of sunshine. The door beyond was open and behind it was a picture of a country landscape, ten feet wide and five feet high. Her mother had bought it thirty years before but, when she got it home, she hated it so much it was banished to the bottom of the house where it would be viewed only in passing. In the corner was a little girl in a blue dress, picking flowers, a garland of daisies around her neck. Alison stroked her finger across the girl, as she had done ten thousand times before. *Hello me.* The house already smelled stale and musty. Go in, go in. Gather the ghosts of history, memories anterior.

'Get that snarl out of your voice, boy.'

It wasn't a snarl, dad. I never snarled. Not at you, nor anyone. It was frustration, despair. It was disappointment.

'Don't know what the hell you're in such a bloody mood for.'

Because the only time you talk to me is to criticise. Because you never consider my feelings. Because I'm treated like shit by a shit like you.

'You see? No answer. Nothin at all.'

No, dad. No answer. Because I was no longer there.

Sandy Disdain most probably died in his sleep, Danny Mills said. Neighbours were alerted by the dog barking. After three hours they ventured in and found him dead in his chair. Alison listened uncomprehendingly. It seemed too outrageous to be true. Fathers are indestructible. Especially hers, the old bastard.

'Toughen yourself up. You'll never be anything in life if you don't learn to look after yourself.'

But wasn't that your job, dad? At least till I could grow up?

Hand on the banister, she steeled herself and turned and let out an involuntary cry. Nothing had changed. The wallpaper, red-brown and gaudily patterned, that carpet with black spirals on a vicious red background. The edges where it had frayed. She remembered when her father had laid it, thirty years before. She remembered the last time she had walked down it, suitcase in hand, future before her. Twenty years later, how small that future seemed. She walked up the stairs, scarcely breathing. The papier-mache pig with no snout was still on guard from the back of the widest step, on the corner. Two plaster dogs stared inwards from the ledge of the giant central window, almost but not quite a pair, almost but not quite valuable. The balusters austerely white, elongated and vaguely pained like Giacometti figures. She recalled there was one whose head was missing. Yes, there it was, on the corner. Alison could never fathom how that might have happened. The stair turned through one hundred and eighty degrees and she could see that the central landing, too, was completely untouched since she had lived there, dark like a contusion. Alison was sucked into anotherwhere, an everytime. She walked into the kitchen, clinical blue walls casting an icy pallor across the room, those huge cupboards her father had built into the wall nearest the door, central table with four chairs. Belfast sink before the window that overlooked the road. Her mother's stool, her resting place while potatoes boiled. Here she used to sing *The Old Rugged Cross* and *Danny Boy* as expertly as any professional.

Peering into the unchanged house was like being an observer of her own history. Noise, feet cascading down the stairs, the Light Programme, her dad's voice thundering. Karen hiding from him in her secret place, writing, always writing. Mum in the kitchen, always alone. Next to the kitchen was the family living room, place of congregation and confrontation, place of punishment, place of anger. Opposite was the bathroom and the blue room, special space for visitors only. Beside the stairs was the toilet and then, in the corner, her parents' bedroom. Upstairs another landing and the bedrooms off it, hers and Karen's. Poor, beautiful Karen. Distorted sounds and smells overtook her, the past funnelling into the present. *Not now. Not yet. Please.* She turned back to the bathroom. On a shelf beside the sink was her father's razor, long and silver, the handle elegantly criss-crossed to improve its grip and, beside it, bristles worn almost to stumps, his shaving brush. The boy Alistair used them when his father was out to shave the downy hairs from his legs and arms and upper lip. Alison closed her eyes. It is always the humblest ghosts that overwhelm. She was back on the road almost before she knew it, blood pounding in her head. Her hands were cold, her brow clammy. She could see her father, that contemptuous look of his. She could smell him. She could hear his voice. And yet, as had always been the way, she couldn't confront him.

That would have to wait.

*

Tuesday morning, nine am, Alison readied herself to confront the registrar. Words of sympathy, sad time, condolence. Alison Disdain, only *compos mentis* kin, responsible adult signing off the death of a man she hadn't seen in twenty years. Alison Disdain, head of the family.

She had forgotten how far out of town Barnkittock was. Could they have made a less accessible place for a registrar's office? She walked slowly. When she finally arrived she could see, a little further ahead, Craigard Road on the right, steep uphill. At the top was Richmond House. In Richmond House was the husk of her mother.

'Miss Disdain,' said the registrar. He explained the process, showed her the paperwork, said it wouldn't take long. Professional demeanour, quiet, efficient, assured, put the mourners at their ease.

'I'll need some identification from you as well,' he said. 'Birth certificate, preferably.'

'You don't, do you?'

'I do, yes.'

'I don't have a birth certificate.'

'We all have a birth certificate. If you've lost it we can replace it. There will be a charge.'

Alison stared at him. She opened her handbag and pulled out a yellowing form. The registrar pointed.

'That's it,' he said.

'No it isn't.' She handed it to him. He read the certificate, in the name of Alistair Disdain. He looked at Alison. 'A person can change their sex,' she said, 'but they're not allowed to change their birth certificate. It's a form of state-sponsored cruelty.'

The registrar swallowed. 'That's correct,' he said. 'I didn't realise.' He stroked the paper for a moment. 'I can process this for you, Miss… I can process this for you, but you will have to sign it in the name that is on this form.'

'That person doesn't exist.'

'In the eyes of the law, that person does exist.'

'And I don't?'

'I don't make the law.'

'Yes, you do. We all do. The law reflects what society

believes.'

'I'm sorry. If you would care to sign, we can complete the paperwork?'

*

There were four mourners at the funeral of Alexander Muir Disdain, 1912–1985. Alison Disdain sat alone on the front row, body stiff with concentration. Each taking a separate pew, her old school friend Jack Duguid, Bob Kelly from Cloudland and Gav Pettigrew from John Low's Fishmonger's sat on the right hand aisle of St Michael's Church. At the back, Danny Mills and his two sons stood with arms held across their stomachs. Reverend Flack, who had never met Sandy Disdain, gave a short address drawn from his brief conversation with Alison the night before.

'It is a truth,' he said, 'that some people make their way in the world garnering few friends. All of us have flaws, some more than others, and that is certainly true of Sandy Disdain. But this is a time for reflection on that which was good. Sandy Disdain was a husband to Mary. He was a father to Alison and to Karen. He came late to fatherhood. He was a man who tried always to do the best. He was from a different age, growing up in poverty after the Great War and having to forge a living for a fatherless family in the hard years that followed, while barely more than a child himself. That fuelled a strong work ethic that never left him. An outdoorsman, he was never comfortable with constraints or conventions or duties. But speak to him on a summer's afternoon, striding the hills around Crieff while he pointed out plants and birds and animals, and you knew what a sharp mind he had, what a quiet, almost secret delight he took in the world, what enthusiasm burned inside him. Sandy Disdain was an autodidact as solitary and self-contained as it's possible to be. He found making friendships impossibly difficult. Emotions were things best kept concealed. Life was lived at a distance. That diffidence left a mark on his relationships with people. Even his own family. Karen, of course, died tragically young. In the wake of that, Alison left home at eighteen and never returned. 'But,' she told me last night, 'the love never dies.' In life we endure much pain and sadness. But there is goodness, too, always there is goodness, often unnoticed at the time. So when you think of Sandy Disdain, I ask you to think of a summer afternoon, of sunshine and warmth, nature all around, and of a good man struggling to reach a compromise with life.'

Alison lowered her head. *The love never dies.* She did say that, yes. What she did not say to Reverend Flack, an honest man and kind, was that her hatred of her father reached a thousand fathoms higher and a thousand fathoms deeper than that love. And it was as dense as existence itself. She stared at the coffin, tried to picture the man within.

Stay there.

*

That evening, her last before rejoining her own life, Alison stared at a hotel wall that was as blank as a rebuke. It felt strange, being home but not home, back in Crieff but not in Dallerie. It hurt that images of Karen were so hard to conjure. She had long, blonde hair, blue eyes, a button nose, full red lips, nice teeth, the smallest ears, small hands, lovely soft skin, her legs foal-like and mostly out of control. Alison remembered all these details individually but she could not combine them into a picture of her sister. Sometimes, unbidden, Karen would appear in her mind, a frozen carbon from a long forgotten moment, laughing in a paddling pool or posing on one leg, arms outstretched or walking to church with a large, knitted tammy covering her head and a duffle coat and white socks and black plastic shoes. The image would disappear before Alison had a chance to interrogate it. It would disappear and each time it disappeared it took longer to return. Where do they go? How to find that parallel track where all still unfolds?

'Your father was found dead at ten forty-five this morning. I thought you'd want to know.'

I thought you'd want to know. How cold that sounded, the call from the police. How distant, unfeeling. But the question remained: did she want to know? She'd asked her father once, years ago, how many animals he'd killed in his life. She had never forgotten the tone of the gamekeeper's reply. It elicited neither pride nor satisfaction, nor shock nor disgust. The banality of the response haunted her. 'Thirty a day for twenty-odd years, probably. Conservative estimate.' She didn't want to calculate it, but she did – over two hundred thousand souls.

Did he remember that, she asked herself yet again. Did he remember that when he wrote the letter? She pulled it out of her bag and opened it, cheap paper completely filled with her father's elaborate, almost unreadable scrawl. Her one and only letter from him. Not even birthday cards, never a Christmas card, no written communication until this letter had arrived a week before he died. She hadn't even known he knew her address. Dear Alistair, it began. Dear Alistair. Dear Alistair.

Her eyes glossed over most of it, details about her mother and her treatment, about the house, his so-called retirement. She skimmed to the end, to the gamekeeper's final confession to his only son.

'I've killed too many things in my life.'

Regret, the most painful emotion of them all. The sinking knowledge of what is done and cannot be undone. Alison folded the letter and put it in its envelope. She looked at herself in the mirror.

'I've killed some things in my life, too.'

*

The following morning, Alison leaned against the Indicator at the top of the Knock hill and watched the dawn. Best view in the world. Once, her father had taught her the names of the hills arrayed around her. She could hear the gruffness of his voice. Only now, twenty years too late, could she hear the need. Reply. Connect. In her head a tune played in an endless loop, *Bourbon and Tears Rag*.

Slow and ponderous it started, offering no glimpse of the emotion to follow, waiting for a modest half beat before settling into the first phase. Then that aching, hopeful, mournful melody, first four bars rising, last four falling, then repeating as though to emphasise the point, hope and loss, hope and loss, hope and loss in 2/4 time. It's the natural rhythm of the end of a life.

She opened the casket and looked inside. Residue. Like a farmer scything corn she released the ashes into the air, casting once, twice, three times, four and five. They caught in the wind and broadcast themselves and scattered and fell and on July the thirtieth, 1985 Sandy Disdain was finally at rest.

*

The room was long and narrow, more like a corridor, with windows running the extent of it, looking out on a sloping garden, lawns and rose beds and, at the bottom, beech and oak trees. Beyond, if the clouds had permitted it, the Ochils and Turleum. A television, bolted high on the far wall, blared an afternoon repeat of *The Love Boat*. From a gaggle of chairs dotted beneath, inhabitants stared up at the enchanter. A long row of chairs faced the garden. Each was populated by some remnant of the Edwardian age. Women outnumbered men nine to one. Nurses in green tunics and black skirts walked briskly or sat stroking a crone's hand. Into this scene of human desolation tottered a younger woman, early sixties only, holding on to a nurse as though fearing evanescence.

Alison watched her approach, sick with apprehension.

'Here we are,' said the nurse, speaking too loudly. She ushered the woman to a high-backed chair next to Alison and guided her into it backwards. The woman settled herself. She looked out of the window at the garden and turned and smiled at Alison and looked out of the window again.

'Wha's that man on that roof up there?'

Alison looked. There was no building, no roof. 'Probably the chimney sweep.'

'It's not Bill Tracey.'

'This person has come to visit you, Mary. Say hello.'

'You're very pretty.'

'Thank you.'

'You look like my Alistair.'

'I'll leave you two alone now.'

'Thank you.'

'Wha's that man on that roof up there? What's he doin?'

'Do you know about your husband? Sandy Disdain?'

'Sandy Disdain. He's my man.'

'Do you know what happened to him?'

'He'll be back for his tea soon. I'm doin mince and tatties the nicht. He likes his mince and tatties.'

'He's dead, mum.'

'Wha are you again?'

'I'm Alistair.' She took the older woman's hand, soft and dry, almost desiccated. Such lovely skin, though, she always had lovely skin. 'I scattered his ashes this morning. Up the Knock. I think he'd have liked that.'

'I'll need to put the water on for the tatties in a minute. Dinnae let me forget.'

'Do you remember Karen?'

'Karen?' The woman's face broke into a smile, childlike and intense, but it disappeared almost immediately, replaced by crumpled disappointment. An instant of connection, deepest pain provoking the last semblance of memory. Then it vanished. Daughter dead, memory voided.

'Wha's that man on that roof up there?'

'I love you, mum.'

'I love you, too, Alistair. Silly laddie.' She continued to stare out at the garden, her expression composed and serene.

'What?'

'I'll be needin to get the water on soon. My man'll be wantin his mince and tatties. He works far ower hard. Isn't that a lovely day? It's like spring. The daffies'll be oot soon. Wha are you again, love? Are you Edith McClelland's lassie? She's a nice lassie, always a good word to say to you. What was her name again? Wha's that man on that roof up there?'

Alison fought back tears. She stroked her mother's hand with her index finger. The old woman looked down at it in surprise and then gave a beatific smile once more.

'That's a bonny frock you have on. Did you mak it yoursel?'

Alison stood up and bent over her mother. She touched her cheek and then kissed it lightly.

'Goodbye, mum.' She turned towards the waiting nurse. She felt the urge to look back, one more time, last glance to fix in the memory, but she fought it because she knew that her mother was not there.

Whisky Night

At seven in the morning on the Monday after the old man's death Ash Harker cycled to the Colony. The old man had snared the lower fields, probably on the Friday morning. Half a dozen rabbits were stiff with rigor mortis, eyes gone, flesh ripped by crows. A couple were already maggoted. The American girl released them and threw them into a ditch and picked up the snares. Four rabbits were still fresh, one alive. She despatched it and gutted them all and piled them into her bag.

She proceeded methodically, trying to free her mind of thought. It didn't work. She kept seeing how the old man would have done it, the deft way he could gut a rabbit with a couple of flicks of the knife and a single delve with his hand, the ease with which he could pull a snare from the ground. She tried not to think about his death. He'd been found sitting in his chair beside the fire. Did he know what was happening? Did he wake up, helpless, alone, afraid? Did he suffer? The moment – her vision of the moment – kept replaying itself in her mind. A final breath, then nothingness. Anyone who reckons time is a once-only event knows jack-shit, she thought. Some moments never end, eternal recurrence as long as there's someone to remember, to care. *He died in his sleep, never felt nothin. Stands to reason.* But the visions she had were not like that and she would not be reassured. Not knowing the truth was like a pain in her heart. What did he do? What did he think?

Did he think about me?

She knew the question was impertinent, a vanity, unworthy of her or of him. To measure a life in relation to your own was cheap. The thought, though, could not be erased.

Damp seeped up her trouser legs. Rain fell on her head and back, gradually working through her clothing onto her flesh. Wetness made her hands cold – *how ridiculous, the middle of July and I'm cold. The old man wouldn't have noticed but I do, goddamnit.* She collected around forty snares and reckoned there were probably another ten somewhere. She kept looking for an hour and gave up.

At John Low's, she refused to take any money for the rabbits. 'They all's his, not mine.' Half an hour later, she found herself at Dallerie without any conscious decision to go there. The old man's house was locked and dark, as though frozen in time. His last moments were here, his last sights these. Part of her wanted to believe he had indeed died in his sleep, but another part refused to believe his last moments were passive. Not him, not that man, that fighter. She refused to believe he would succumb. She refused to believe he was dead.

But he was.

Why did I come here? she thought.

Because I'm lonely, she answered. It struck her like a revelation and she resolved never to be lonely again. It was a vulnerability that others could use against her, a flaw that threatened her independence. *It's jes me, me against the world, and the world don't care dipshit bout me so I don't care dipshit bout it.*

That was the litany. Now, she had to make herself believe it.

She gazed up at the house one last time and walked away without looking back. New world, new plan. The afternoon had faired up, a slight sun shining down and the air warm on her skin. She walked along the Academy playing fields and through the railway embankment and made her way down to the river and peace and solitude. Lady Mary's Walk stretched in front of her, straight and wide, beech-lined on either side, the tree tops coming together to form a canopy. Beneath, it was dark and cool, the ground soft from generations of leaf-fall dissolving into humus. Alongside, the river Earn ran serene and quiet except for patches of turmoil where giant rocks impeded its flow. The water crashed over and round these obstructions, that which was peaceful suddenly roused into agitation. Hidden violence. Latent power.

She found the broken-down fence lining the ghost of the old railway line and counted back to the third tree on the left and walked around it, trailing her hand across its rough bark. Carved into it were initials and names of the lovers and children of Crieff across generations, as they were on every tree in turn, old Crieff custom, parish register of the poor and hopeful over decades. She found the entries she sought.

AD

19/8/46

And:

KD

21/6/47

She traced her finger around the markings, seeking a connection with the man who carved them nearly forty years before. The old man, then a young man, what hopes did he have for those children, Alistair and Karen Disdain? What life did he imagine for them? For himself? If he had known how it would end, what would he have done differently? Could he have?

'Can I?' she said aloud. No answer was returned.

Above the children's initials there was a larger, older engraving of a heart, beautifully carved, symmetrical. Inside were the initials:

SD & MK

21/8/45

Sandy Disdain and Mary Kemp, married to celebrate the end of war, the return to normality. Whatever normality might be.

Ash felt in her jeans and pulled out her penknife. She chose a spot beside the old man's heart and slowly, carefully, began to carve her own, identical in size and shape, cutting deep and true. She laboured over it for half an hour, making it perfect. When it was done she stood back. There was room inside for initials but she had no initials to include. Who was Ash Harker? Where did she belong? What was her destination? When she was with the old man she had felt, for the first time, solidarity, purpose, companionship. What did she feel now?

Hollow.

Ash had never cried in her life, not even when her momma died, but at that moment, solitary in lovers' lane, a seeker lost, she came close. She walked into town and in the Cooperative she bought bread and stole whisky and slowly she climbed through town to Ferntower. She spoke to no-one.

The lonely hunter let herself into the howff and placed the whisky bottle on the table. She took a tumbler from the cupboard and filled it and sat down. She stared at the old man's chair through the gloom. It was like a void in time.

'I'm gonna snare the high fields at Culcrieff tomorrow,' she said aloud. 'I figure it's a while since you last did em. And, soon as I find where you keep your nets, I'm gonna have a run through up at the Colony. Saw a field there today looked jes right.'

Silence encased her. A chill went through her. She took her fiddle and placed it low on her shoulder and she began to play and she began to sing.

> Did you hear that lonesome whippoorwill?
> He sounds too blue to fly.
> The midnight train is whining low
> And I'm so lonesome I could cry.

She sipped her whisky and closed her eyes. His aroma was all around, so strong she figured if she kept her eyes shut long enough when she opened them he'd be there. She tried. His empty chair loomed before her. She stood up and looked outside at the evening darkness. How can he not be here, when every molecule of air in this room has cycled through his body a thousand times? When does a space and its occupants merge? When do they divide? She grabbed the whisky bottle and sat down again, stretching almost horizontal. The darkness soothed her. This evening she would be alone. This evening she would remember. She would mourn.

Whisky night.

And, in the morning, when the dawn comes and the birds start to sing and the world to turn, life would resume because that is the only way it knows how.

About the Stories

Fair Near a Riverside Town was shortlisted in the London Independent Story Prize competition in 2020. It is an adapted extract from an as yet unpublished novel, Cloudland.

(In My Way) won second prize in the Flash 500 Short Story Competition in 2017.

Burials was the winner of the ChipLit Festival Short Story Competition in 2018 and was described by judge Rachel Seiffert as 'dark and well-crafted'.

Fresh Watter was published in Break In Case of Silence: New Writing Scotland Volume 39 in 2021 and has previously been shortlisted for the ChipLit and Exeter Story Prizes. It is a prequel to the Bob Kelty series of historical crime novels, introducing Bob as a young child.

The Entertainer won the Enizagam Writing Competition in 2019 and was previously published in Enizagam Literary Journal. It is based on characters from Cloudland.

A Curious Judgement is set in 1832, a febrile time which saw significant (and long overdue) changes in the governance of the United Kingdom, including the Great Reform Act and an act removing the death penalty for relatively minor offences such as sheep stealing.

Brainspotting came from a writing exercise as part of my MA in Creative Writing at University of Hull. It is a parody of Irvine Welsh's Trainspotting.

Joss'n'Jules Forever won the Bedford International Writing Prize in 2019 and was previously published in the Bedford International Writing Prize Anthology the same year. It is an adapted extract from Cloudland.

Peewit won third place in the HISSAC Flash Fiction competition in 2018. It is an adapted extract from Cloudland.

Sequela was highly commended in the HISSAC Flash Fiction competition in 2018. It is based on characters from Cloudland.

The Rational Matters of Rational Men is inspired by the writings of the great Affleck Gray (although Jock Menzies is assuredly not based on Affleck).

Man Walks Into A Bar won the HISSAC Flash Fiction Competition in 2017. The judges described it as a "hugely impressive piece of work. Rarely will you read a piece of Flash Fiction that gets so much into such a short space".

The White Deer was shortlisted in the Evesham Festival of Words Short Story Competition in 2019.

The Woman Who Called Herself Karen is based on characters from Cloudland.

Taking Tea With The Other Woman has been shortlisted in a number of short story competitions, including the Ruth Rendell Competition in 2018.

Not Drowning Yet was highly commended in the MTP Short Story competition in 2019. It is based on characters from Cloudland.

The Weight of Snow was shortlisted for the Bedford International Writing Prize in 2019.

Oysters and Ink was shortlisted in the Segora Short Story Competition in 2019. It is based on characters from Cloudland.

Evanescence is adapted and based on characters from Cloudland.

Whisky Night won first prize in the Writing Magazine competition in February 2018. The judges described it as a 'tour de force of accumulated impressions and heightened perceptions'. It is an adapted extract from Cloudland.

Acknowledgements

The majority of these stories have their genesis in a period when I was a member of an online writing group, Alex Keegan's Bootcamp (alongside such writers as CL Taylor, Dan Malakin and Vanessa Gebbie). Bootcamp was a difficult place, with a furious work ethic and a tendency towards brutal honesty in critiques. It wasn't for the faint-hearted, but my experience in Bootcamp made me the writer I am, and I am hugely grateful to Alex Keegan for his inspirational (if sometimes uncomfortable) tutoring. I am also grateful to all my fellow Bootcampers, for their support and kindness. Together, we proved that sometimes you really can polish a turd.

As ever, I have had brilliant support from my team at Ringwood Publishing, under the expert guidance of Sandy Jamieson and Isobel Freeman. My editor, Andrew Mackenzie, has done his usual excellent job, ably assisted by Anna Salomó. Thank you very much to both of them for making this fun.

During the past year I gave up working in local government and started as a full-time writer. My thanks, as always, to my wonderful partner Jackie Pitcher for putting up with me padding downstairs every hour to make a fresh cup of tea and playing John Coltrane a fraction too loud for human comfort.

And, naturally, thank you to you, my readers. If you enjoyed the stories in this collection, please go on to Amazon, Good Reads and Facebook and tell everyone (and me) that you did. Word-of-mouth recommendations make a huge difference.

And I'll see you all in a few months, with Barvick Falls, the latest adventure for Bob and Annie (and Ellen, although you don't know Ellen yet).

About the Author

Rob McInroy was born in Crieff, Perthshire and his writing is all set in his home county, particularly Crieff, the Knock Hill and the River Earn.

In 2018 he was a winner of the Bradford Literature Festival Northern Noir Crime Novel competition and his first novel (Cuddies Strip) was subsequently longlisted for the CWA John Creasey First Blood Dagger Award for best debut novel in 2020. It was acclaimed by Val McDermid as "Highly Recommended" due to its contemporary resonances. McInroy followed this with Barossa Street, and most recently, Moot, published by Ringwood in early 2024.

Rob McInroy is the previous winner of four short story competitions (Hissac, ChipLit Fest, Writing Magazine and the Bedford International Writing Competition), and has been shortlisted for a further sixteen. Rob also holds an MA in Creative Writing, and a PHD in American Literature, both from the University of Hull.

He currently lives in Yorkshire.

www.facebook.com/muirtonenclosurepress

www.twitter.com/McInRob

www.robmcinroy.co.uk

By the same author:

Cuddies Strip

Two young sweethearts, Danny Kerrigan and Marjory Fenwick, walk home along the Cuddies Strip, a lover's lane on the outskirts of Perth. Suddenly, two shots ring out.

Eighteen-year-old Danny slumps to the ground. Seventeen-year-old Marjory flees, but is chased, caught, and brutally assaulted. What follows is an investigation which shook the quiet city of Perth.

Longlisted for the CWA Daggers first novel award, Winner of the Bradford Literature Festival Northern Noir crime novel award. Chosen by Val McDermid as one of three top picks for new crime fiction at Bloody Scotland 2021.

ISBN: 978-1-901514-88-9
£9.99

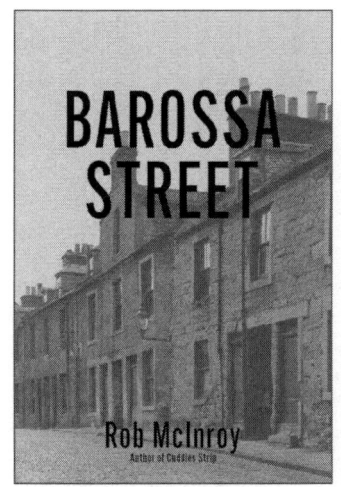

ISBN: 978-1-901514-41-4
£9.99

Barossa Street

Barossa Street follows Cuddies Strip's protagonist, Bob Kelty, as he winds up in the throes of another gruesome murder case. He runs into an old friend with an urgent request and his desire to seek justice gets the better of him. Along with his girlfriend Annie, he takes on the task of tracking down the real killer, and clearing the name of his old friend.

Set in Perth, *Barossa Street* offers not only a look at the mishandling of justice in the face of 1930's prejudice, but also serves as a commentary of the British public's response to the government's shortcomings.

Moot

July 1939, and 3,500 young men from around the world arrive at Monzie Castle in Perthshire for the third international Rover Scout Moot. In the shadow of looming war the Moot seems to be a last gasp of international friendship and fraternity. But among them is a murderer.

Bob Kelty discovers a dead body in a burnt-out tent on the edge of the camp. He is immediately suspicious but for some reason the authorities seem reluctant to become involved.

And if the authorities won't look into them, Bob decides he must. And the question is: when is a murder not a murder?

ISBN: 978-1-917011-00-6

£12.99

If you enjoyed *Burials* you may like these other Ringwood books:

ISBN: 978-1-917011-02-0

£12.99

Song of the Stag
R. M. Brown

Cait and her childhood sweetheart, Kenzie, are from Storran's borders: idyllic, traditional and completely opposed to separatism.

When Kenzie is called up to the ranks of the Queen's Watch to hunt down Storrian Separatists, they move together to the city of Thorterknock, where Cait quickly realises that her charming countryside life is not the reality for every citizen of Storran. Struggle abounds on the cobbled streets, as does the battle for Storran's liberation from the Five Realms.

Cait finds herself swept into a struggle for freedom, with Kenzie and the Queen's Watch on one side, and the Fox and the Separatists on the other.

Remember the Rowan
Kirsten MacQuarrie

Poet Kathleen Raine is initially unimpressed when she meets Gavin Maxwell, a would-be portrait painter struggling to recover from a recent breakdown. Nevertheless, the pair soon bond over a mysterious vision they share of a rowan tree.

They share a cottage in the wildest reaches of the West Highlands, where they care for Gavin's beloved pet otter Mij and for each other. But when tragedy strikes, love soon turns to hate, and Kathleen finds herself being written out of her own life. *Remember the Rowan* shines a light on the woman behind Ring of Bright Water.

ISBN: 978-1-917011-04-4
£12.99

Kitten Heels
Maureen Cullen

Kathleen Gallagher is resourceful, brave and tireless — but fated to work in the bra factory like her mother. It's 1962, and Kathleen resents her situation. She has to look after her three younger siblings and sacrifice her social life for responsibilities she never asked for. When Kathleen's grandmother dies, the entire family dynamic changes — leaving the relationship with her mother to suffer.

ISBN: 978-1-917011-01-3
£9.99

Kitten Heels is a moving coming-of-age story, set in 1960s working class Clydeside and told from thirteen-year-old Kathleen's perspective. Dealing with issues of poverty, mental health, and the role of women, Kitten Heels follows Kathleen as she finds comfort and support in the community of women around her — learning from the way in which these women find ways to grow, nourish and heal each other, despite hardships and institutional obstacles set in their way.